pitch black

color me lost

melody carlson

NAVPRESS
Discipleship Inside Out

THINK

NAVPRESS

Discipleship Inside Out™

NavPress is the publishing ministry of The Navigators, an international Christian organization and leader in personal spiritual development. NavPress is committed to helping people grow spiritually and enjoy lives of meaning and hope through personal and group resources that are biblically rooted, culturally relevant, and highly practical.

For a free catalog go to www.NavPress.com
or call 1.800.366.7788 in the United States or 1.800.839.4769 in Canada.

TH1NK and the TH1NK logo are registered trademarks of NavPress. Absence of ® in connection with marks of NavPress or other parties does not indicate an absence of registration of those marks.

ISBN 978-1-57683-532-6

Cover design by David Carlson Design
Cover photograph by Comstock Images
Creative Team: Gabe Filkey s.c.m., Erin Healy, Arvid Wallen, Kathy Mosier, Glynese Northam

This is a work of fiction. The characters, incidents, and dialogues are products of the author's imagination and are not to be construed as real. Any resemblance to actual events or persons, living or dead, is entirely coincidental.

Published in association with the literary agency of Sara A. Fortenberry.

Scripture taken from THE MESSAGE (MSG). Copyright © 1993, 1994, 1995, 1996, 2000, 2001, 2002. Used by permission of NavPress Publishing Group; and the New King James Version (NKJV). Copyright © 1982 by Thomas Nelson, Inc. Used by permission. All rights reserved.

Carlson, Melody.
    Pitch black : color me lost / Melody Carlson.-- 1st ed.
        p. cm. -- (TrueColors ; bk. 4)
    Summary: After one of their classmates kills himself, seventeen-year-old Morgan, whose faith in God was already wavering, makes a suicide pact with some other students.
    ISBN 1-57683-532-4
    [1. Suicide--Fiction. 2. Christian life--Fiction. 3. High schools--Fiction.
4. Schools--Fiction.] I. Title.
    PZ7.C216637Pi 2004
    [Fic]--dc22
                                                    2004018639

Printed in the United States of America

7 8 9 10 11 12 / 15 14

Other Books by Melody Carlson

Harsh Pink (NavPress)

Moon White (NavPress)

Bright Purple (NavPress)

Faded Denim (NavPress)

Bitter Rose (NavPress)

Blade Silver (NavPress)

Fool's Gold (NavPress)

Burnt Orange (NavPress)

Torch Red (NavPress)

Deep Green (NavPress)

Dark Blue (NavPress)

DIARY OF A TEENAGE GIRL *series* (Multnomah)

DEGREES *series* (Tyndale)

Crystal Lies (WaterBrook)

Finding Alice (WaterBrook)

Three Days (Baker)

On This Day (WaterBrook)

one

"*DID YOU HEAR ABOUT JASON?*" CARLIE'S EYES ARE HUGE AS SHE GRABS ME by the arm. But I'm not in the mood for her theatrics right now. And I'm not interested in hearing the latest juicy bits of gossip. Not even about Jason.

Ignoring her, I slam my messy locker shut. A sleeve of my favorite red sweatshirt is dangling out, hanging there like a panting tongue, begging to be rescued. But I just give the metal door a loud kick and turn away.

"Morgan!" Carlie is glaring at me now. "Listen to me—"

"*Just leave me alone!*" I snap at her. "I'm going to be late for economics." Then I shake free from her grip and just walk away. Okay, I know I'm being totally rude right now. And Carlie used to be my best friend. I should turn around and apologize to her, because friends don't treat friends like this. And, considering that my friends are pretty limited these days (like I can easily count them on one hand with fingers left over), I should really know better than to act like this.

But the fact is, I just don't care. Because this is reality: My life sucks. And I am totally fed up. So everyone will be much better off if they just leave Morgan Bergstrom alone. At least for a while.

It's like I can't see anyone as I storm down the hallway toward the east wing. I feel like I'm walking down this dark tunnel, fueled by anger. Oh, I sort of sense the voices around me. And I can tell that kids are here and there, and maybe they're even looking at me. But like I said, I just don't care anymore. I've got bigger problems to consider right now.

Tell me this: How can I be expected to get out of bed every morning and show up at this moronic school in order to get a stupid education (which is probably totally worthless) when everything in my life is totally out of control? I mean, seriously, how much does a seventeen-year-old girl have to take?

It's not like this latest mess is my fault either. I mean, I've tried to do my best, make good choices, even be fairly responsible. And for what? Everything in my life just keeps falling apart. Everything's unraveling and I just can't take it anymore.

Okay, it's no big deal that my parents got divorced when I was in grade school. That happens to lots of kids. And eventually you get over it. Or so you tell yourself. And never mind that my older brother, Jonathan, is using drugs and my mom is totally oblivious. He hardly ever comes home anyway, although every time he does, something valuable disappears. Last time he took my CD player. I now have a dead bolt on my bedroom door. But that's not really the problem.

I admit it bugs me that my mom doesn't really seem to notice these things lately (like Jonathan's addiction problem). And even if I try to tell her, she's so preoccupied with her own life that she doesn't really listen. Oh, she pretends to listen, but you can tell by that glazed-over, dreamy look in her eyes that she's off in la-la land thinking about *Bradley*. Stupid, moronic Bradley Finch! Man, I wish she'd never met this loser from her job at SPUD (Stanton Public Utility Department). In my opinion, Bradley is a SPUD dud.

But they've been dating for a couple of months now, and it's like he's launched my normally somewhat-conservative mom into this ridiculous middle-aged pursuit of youth and superficiality. Not only is it totally embarrassing (I mean, you should see what she's *wearing* lately) but it's completely ruining our lives. Talk about a train wreck!

It doesn't help anything that Bradley is in his twenties (he won't tell us his actual age) and my mom is forty-three (which she won't admit to Bradley). She even told him that she'd had her kids when she was "just a kid" herself, which is totally bogus, not to mention lame. But it's like she suddenly thinks she's Demi Moore and he's Ashton Kutcher and they are the hottest couple in town. Give me a break!

At first I told myself to just chill, that this whole thing would blow over before Valentine's Day. Most of my mom's romances don't last more than twenty minutes anyway, and this one seemed more doomed than the others. So I figured if I could keep my mouth shut and just be patient, things would eventually return to normal. Or at least as normal as they can be in our house.

Okay, so maybe I was delusional. Because Valentine's Day has come and gone and it's just a week before spring break, and this guy is not leaving anytime soon. And now I'm even blaming myself, like maybe I could've done something to prevent it from going any further. But, stupid me, I thought their relationship was too ridiculous to be taken seriously. That is, until last night when those two idiots took their stupidity to a whole new level.

"We're getting married!" my mom announced from where the two lovebirds were snuggled up together on our couch. Now, she said this like it was *really good news*, like I should jump up and down for joy. Yeah, you wish.

"What?" I demanded, actually hoping that I'd heard her wrong.

She smiled at me and laid a big wet one on Bradley's cheek. Then, giggling like she was in middle school, she turned back to me. "We're in love, honey. We've decided to get married."

"Married?" I actually gasped now. I mean, it was one thing for them to date, and I know that Bradley has been spending the night here in our house. But marriage? Right.

"We love each other, Morgan. Can't you see that?"

"But, Mom . . ."

"I know, I know . . ." Mom smiled at me in this out-to-lunch sort of way. "It probably seems sudden to you. But we really want to do this."

"When?" I asked in a wimped-out voice.

"We're both taking off work tomorrow. We'll fly standby to Vegas, get married in one of those cute little chapels like Kelly Ripa did, and then we'll have our honeymoon weekend there." She paused to wink at Bradley, as if she thinks I don't know that they've already had their honeymoon and then some.

I groaned and started to leave.

"Can't you just be happy for me, Morgan?" my mom pleaded in a freaky-sounding little-girl voice.

I felt like I was going to be sick. "Mom," I said in my best grown-up tone, "you can't be serious. I mean, you guys barely know each other. And Bradley is, well, he's a lot younger than—"

"Oh, Morgan." My mom made a pouty face that does not belong on the face of the woman I had respected until recently. "You know that age is just a number."

"But, Mom, what about—"

"Hey, Morgan," Bradley interrupted me, "why don't you just lighten up a little?" He paused to stroke my mom's recently bleached hair. "Can't you see we belong together? Lee Anne's the best thing that's ever happened to me."

I wanted to suggest that perhaps Lee Anne could adopt him, since I felt pretty sure she was old enough to be his mother. Okay, maybe she would've had to have gotten pregnant in high school. But hey, she claims she did that anyway.

"Whatever," I finally said. What difference did my opinion make to those two anyway?

"You'll get used to it," said Bradley. Yeah, right.

"I've got homework," I told them as I headed toward my room.

"So you'll be okay, honey?" my mom called after me as I opened my door.

"Yeah, I'll be perfectly fine." I doubted she noticed the dead sound in my voice.

"And you don't mind being home by yourself for a few days?"

"Don't worry about me," I called as I closed the door to my room, securing the dead bolt even though Jonathan wasn't around. Then I threw myself on my bed and cried. I think I actually hoped that my mom might hear me crying and come in, like she used to, and ask me what was wrong. I thought maybe she'd see how absurd this marriage business was and come to her senses and change her mind about running off with SPUD Dud.

But she didn't. When I got up this morning, she was already gone. Her suitcases were gone. Her car was gone. She didn't even leave a note telling me where she'd be staying or when she'd return. For all I know she might never come back. I'm not even sure I would care. All I know is that my life sucks. And I wonder why I even bothered getting out of bed and dragging myself to this stupid school so I could sit here in this stupid economics class and be bored nearly senseless by this stupid teacher.

I glance around the classroom now, wondering how I even managed to get here and sit down. I can tell by the clock that this class is nearly over, and I don't even remember it starting. It's like I've been stuck in time, or maybe I'm experiencing the twilight zone. But suddenly I remember that Carlie had been trying to tell me something about Jason. I look around the room to see where he's sitting. Maybe my pity party is coming to an end because I now feel slightly curious as to what's up with Jason and why it's so interesting to Carlie.

Maybe he's finally gotten that mongoose tattoo (he keeps saying that he's going to do it someday). Now wouldn't that make his respectable, conservative parents freak out? But I don't see Jason in class. And suddenly I'm wondering if he's gotten into some kind of trouble. I sure hope not, since I'd really like to talk to him today.

Jason and I have been friends since grade school. We even tried going out together when we were fifteen, but it felt too much like I was kissing my brother, and so we called it quits.

"Let's just keep on being good friends," I told him. And he agreed. And that's what we've done. In fact, I'm thinking that Jason is just the guy to pour out my current problems to. He's a way better listener than Carlie, even though he lives in this freakishly perfect world with parents who are still happily married to each other and go to church every Sunday and mow their lawn on Saturdays and have respectable jobs and impressive friends. Considering all that, it's pretty amazing that Jason is so understanding of my whacked-out little life. I actually think he's somewhat fascinated by the weirdness of it, and he'll probably want to hear the whole story of how my mom is eloping with stupid Bradley. Maybe we can have lunch together today.

Sometimes I wonder why Jason's been such a loyal friend to me.

I think it might be because he considers himself the black sheep of his family. Which is totally ridiculous, since Jason is the coolest and most together guy I know. He gets good grades, goes out for sports, hardly ever gets into trouble, and if he does, he's always sorry afterward. Sure, he's not perfect, but compared to most kids, he's got a lot going for him.

Of course, he doesn't see it that way at all. But I think it's just because he compares himself to his older brother and sister (who must be directly descended from God, they are so disgustingly perfect). It's a lot to live up to, and sometimes Jason gets discouraged. And that's when he tends to do things that aren't so smart. Things he later regrets. Like the time he wrecked his dad's classic Mustang drag racing down by the lake. Not a good scene. But he worked all summer to help pay off the insurance deductible, and eventually he even got to drive again. Although his dad sold the Mustang.

The bell jerks me back to the present and I realize that class is over and I don't even know if we were assigned homework. I gather up my stuff, shove it into my bag, and head for the door.

"Morgan," says Alyssa Reynolds in this sympathetic tone that makes me uneasy. I mean, this girl doesn't really like me and everyone knows she can be a total witch sometimes. *"How are you doing?"*

"Huh?" I look at her and wonder if she's suddenly turned psychic or nice or both. How could she possibly know about my mom and Bradley? I haven't even told Carlie yet. "What do you mean?" I ask.

"I mean about Jason." She puts her hand on my arm and I feel this icy chill rush through me. Like I know deep down inside that something is wrong. Really wrong.

"What do you mean *about Jason*?" My voice sounds abnormally high-pitched now.

"You haven't heard?"

"What's wrong, Alyssa?" I can see other kids gathering around us now, like maybe they all know something I don't. "What's wrong?" I say again. "What's going on?"

"Oh, I just assumed you knew." She looks uncomfortable now.

"Knew *what*?" My voice is getting louder.

She frowns. "Oh, Morgan, I hate to be the one to tell you."

I grab her by the arm now. *"Just tell me*, Alyssa. What is going on? What happened to Jason?"

"He, uh, he . . ." Her eyes dart to the other kids. "He killed himself last night."

two

I FEEL LIKE SOMEONE HAS JUST SUCKED THE OXYGEN RIGHT OUT OF MY lungs, like I can't catch my breath, or maybe I'm underwater and sinking like a stone.

"No," I finally tell Alyssa. "That can't be true."

She just nods with a sad expression. "I'm sorry, Morgan. I know you guys were close and everything. But it's true."

I turn and stare at the other kids, hoping they will straighten Alyssa out and explain to this ditzy chick that Jason Harding is alive and well and that people shouldn't go around pulling stunts like this. But their expressions seem to mirror Alyssa's. They all have this weird mixture of sadness and confusion and fear on their faces. And some are even crying.

"No," I tell her again. "I don't believe you, Alyssa. If Jason was dead I would know it."

"It's been on the news," says Eric Zimmer. "The whole school knows about it."

"I heard there's a special counselor to talk to kids," offers Eva Fernandez.

"Maybe you should go see him, Morgan," adds Alyssa.

They continue talking to me or at me or about me, I'm not even sure—I can't process what they're saying anymore. It's like these heavy curtains have fallen over my eyes and ears and I can't absorb what's going on around me.

I feel a hand on my elbow as someone guides me somewhere. I try to take in a breath, try to steady myself as I attempt to walk down the hallway in a straight line. I turn to see that it's Eva next to me and she's talking to me as we walk.

I don't really get what she's saying, but the tone of her voice is gentle and calming. And I'm hoping that maybe I've just totally mis-understood everything. I mean, I realize that I wasn't thinking too clearly this morning, and I was really bummed about Mom and Bradley. Maybe I'm just having some sort of a breakdown where reality gets all twisted and distorted. Maybe I just need to take a nap or a pill or throw some cold water on my face.

I remember we're supposed to be having a yearbook meeting after school today. Jason told me about it on Monday, and I know that he wouldn't miss this important meeting that he scheduled himself.

"We're running short on candid shots," he told me as he handed me a bag of film—the old-fashioned kind (35 mm that comes in rolls, since I still stubbornly use my old Nikon that I've had since middle school). "We need you to get a bunch of random photos," he said. "Hopefully get them developed and put onto a disk before spring break."

I remember how I saluted him. "Yes, sir," I said. "Whatever you say, sir." But the truth is, I haven't taken a single photo yet. I had planned to make up for it today. My camera is loaded and in my backpack. I'll cover both the track meet and the ball game. That should make Jason happy.

Suddenly I'm standing in front of the office and I can't even remember how I got here or why. But Eva is standing next to me and she's pointing at something. I look up.

Taped to the wall next to the office is an enlarged photo of Jason. It's his yearbook picture from last year. And whoever blew it up didn't do a very good job. It looks kind of grainy and uneven. But it's obviously Jason. And this confuses me. Why is his picture up there? Maybe he's student of the month, although they don't usually go to this much trouble.

I look beneath the photo to read the computer-generated sign: *"In Loving Memory of Jason Harding. We'll Miss You!"* Beneath that is a long sheet of white butcher paper that goes all around the office wall. It has what appears to be graffiti all over it, but on closer inspection, I can see that kids have written their names along with notes to Jason. But it just doesn't make any sense.

I look at Eva. "This isn't for real, is it?" I ask so quietly that I can hardly even hear myself.

She nods. "I'm sorry, Morgan."

"No." I shake my head and look away. "No, no . . . it can't be . . ."

She puts her hand on my shoulder and I look back up at his photo again. I look into that face that I've known all these years. I look into the eyes that could always see right through me. And I realize as if for the first time that something is really wrong. The grainy photo becomes soft and blurry as my eyes fill with tears and the ache in my chest feels lethal.

And then suddenly, as if I've just been stabbed by the blade of reality, it all becomes painfully clear to me. *Jason must really be dead.* As impossible as this is to wrap my mind around, I think maybe this horrible thing has really happened.

With legs that are beginning to shake uncontrollably, I turn back to Eva. "It's really true?" I ask.

This time she just nods.

And that's when my legs just totally give way and I collapse like a broken doll. I crumple into this pitiful little heap of misery right next to the office door, where I hear phones ringing and voices talking as if nothing whatsoever is wrong. I crouch beneath Jason's grainy photo and burrow my head into my knees and sob.

"Jason, come back," I plead and beg. "Please, Jason, come back. Come back." I say these words over and over, thinking that maybe, if I say them enough or if I wish for it hard enough, just maybe I can undo this awful thing that has stolen my friend away from me. But it's not working because my world is quickly turning black. Pitch black.

three

I DON'T REMEMBER COMING INTO THE HEALTH ROOM, BUT I CAN SEE THAT'S where I am now. I wonder how I know this since I've never actually been in here before. Maybe it's the smell, a combination of dusty vinyl upholstery and disinfectant soap.

"Feeling better?" asks Mrs. Lender, the office lady. She must be about the same age as my mom, but she actually dresses in what seems like the appropriate apparel for a middle-aged woman. Okay, maybe the teacher sweater with red apples on the front is a bit much. She is offering me a paper cup, which I assume must be full of water.

I nod and take the cup, then just look at it, wondering what I am supposed to do with it.

"Drink it," she tells me.

So I do. Then I hand the cup back and just wait.

"Eva said that you just heard about Jason," she says sadly.

"Is it really true?" I ask with the slightest twinge of hope, like maybe I've just been hallucinating.

"Yes. Unfortunately it is. We have a grief counselor on campus today. He's with another student right now, but you could—"

"I don't want to," I say quickly, standing up on what feel like spaghetti legs. "I just—I just want to go home." I look at her with hot tears running down my cheeks again. "Please, can't I just—just go home?"

"Is there someone there you can talk to?" she asks. "To help you process your loss?"

"Sure," I lie. I vaguely wonder what she means by those words. How on earth does anyone *process* something like this?

"Okay, I'll go see what I can do." She hands me a Kleenex box. "Why don't you sit back down and wait here."

I soak several Kleenexes before she comes back. It's like the tears won't stop coming now. And my head is throbbing like a crowd is pounding from the inside with a hundred mini jackhammers.

"You can go home, Morgan. Do you need to use the office phone to call for a ride?"

"No," I manage to say as I stand and pat my backpack. "I've got my cell." Another lie. I am still one of the few kids on the planet without a cell phone.

"Okay, then." She makes a sad little smile. "Take it easy and maybe you'll feel more like yourself by Monday."

"Yeah," I say as I head for the door. I don't even thank her. I just want to get out as quickly as possible and hopefully without seeing any of my friends. I hurry out of the office and straight for the front door, then take off down the sidewalk in the direction of our neighborhood, walking as fast as I can.

I am about four blocks from school, and nearly halfway home, when I remember that I rode my bike to school today. Even so, there is no way I'm going back for it now. I keep heading toward my house in a dazed state of numbness. All I can think about is Jason. And I keep asking myself *why*. Why? Why?

By the time I reach my street, I begin to wonder if this whole thing is really true or not. What if someone got their facts wrong?

Like maybe Jason *tried* to kill himself, but he's still alive? Or what if it was really someone else, someone who's been mistaken for Jason? Couldn't that happen? I think I saw something like that on a TV movie once.

Because really, why would Jason Harding, the coolest guy I know, do himself in? Really, it's totally absurd. Then it occurs to me that maybe he's cooked this whole thing up just to get some weird kind of attention or to make people think.

By the time I reach my front porch steps, I feel certain this is exactly what has happened. Of course, it makes perfect sense. Jason has pulled a really sick joke on everyone—including me!

I fish in my bag for my house key and imagine myself calling Jason and yelling at him for giving me such a freaking scare. But then after I yell at him, I'll tell him that I'm actually very thankful he's alive, and then I'll invite him over here to hang with me today. Hey, we can have the whole place to ourselves and even make a mess if we want to. Maybe we'll order a pizza—pepperoni and olive, just how he likes it—and then we'll find some good pay-per-views and run up my mom's cable bill. Yeah.

But when I go inside, I drop my backpack on the living room floor, kick off my flip-flops, and head straight for my bed. And that's where I crash, crying myself into a fitful sleep where reality and fantasy become so intertwined that by the time I wake up I am not sure about anything. Except that it's nearly four o'clock in the afternoon and I don't know how I could've slept so long.

My head is hot and stuffy and I feel incredibly thirsty, like I've been out in the desert for days. As I go to the kitchen for a glass of water, I try to remember why I'm at home instead of at school, which has already gotten out by now.

Jason. It hits me as I turn on the tap. *Jason is dead.* But even as those words go through my head, I still don't believe them. It's got to be a hoax or a mistake or just a really bad dream. Because I know — *I just know*—that Jason Harding cannot possibly be dead. It's just so wrong.

I watch as the glass fills up, then I drink a few sips of water, but it tastes like metal and suddenly I don't know why I thought I was so thirsty in the first place. I pour the water down the sink and stand there for a long time, just staring down the drain as I wonder what I should do next. It's like I can't even think.

Then I hear a shuffling sound outside the front door, and for some reason I feel certain that it must be Jason. He's come by to straighten this freaky mess up. He's going to tell me that this whole thing is just a moronic misunderstanding, a case of mistaken identity. I run to the door and open it wide. But no one is there. I look out to the street, ready to call out to him, to tell him to come back. But all I see is our paperboy, Kenny Green, pedaling down the street with a bag of newspapers hanging over his shoulder.

That's when I notice the afternoon paper lying on the porch at my feet. I sigh as I stoop to pick it up, disappointed that it wasn't Jason at my door. But even before my hand touches the newspaper, I see the photograph — bold black and white, right on the front page.

I pick it up and stare at one of Jason's senior pictures (he got them back only a couple of weeks ago). But even as I look at it, I tell myself that this isn't for real. I try to convince myself that this is all just part of his elaborate hoax and that I shouldn't be taken in by it. I should know better. Then I go inside.

I close the door and take the newspaper into the living room, where I sit down on the couch and force my eyes to read the headline above his photo. It shouldn't take long for me to see right through this thing. But the headline is not encouraging.

STANTON HIGH SENIOR DIES FROM OVERDOSE

Overdose? Incredulously, I read the word again. Then I continue to read the short article, although it's hard to follow the words because my hands begin to shake so badly.

> Late last night, 18-year-old Jason Harding, son of City Councilor Gary Harding, was transported to Amherst General Hospital, where he died in the early morning hours. The cause of death is listed as liver failure. Sources say Harding ingested a lethal dose of the commonly used painkiller Tylenol (acetaminophen) on Thursday.
>
> Jason Harding was a well-liked senior at Stanton High School. An athlete and honor roll student, he was also managing editor of Stanton High's newspaper and on the yearbook staff. Active in his church youth group and a volunteer coach for SoccerKidz, no one seems to know why this young man would take his life. Harding was . . .

That's all I can take. I let the paper slide down to the floor as I collapse back onto the couch and try to absorb what I've just read. Okay, it must be true. Jason must really be dead. Because there is no way he could fake something like this. And if he really died of an overdose, there's no way it could be a case of mistaken identity either. So it must be true. *Jason really is dead.*

Thinking of Jason like that, lying in a hospital or a morgue or a funeral home or whatever, just cold and not breathing, is absolutely killing me. It feels like someone has dumped a load of cement on top of me and it's crushing the life and breath out of me. This is too much pain.' How can anyone survive this much pain?

four

I'M NOT SURE IF I BLACKED OUT OR WHAT, BUT WHEN I COME TO I FEEL confused and sick. My head is hot and throbbing, but the rest of me feels ice-cold. I shiver. It takes me a minute to remember what is going on, but then I see the newspaper down on the floor with Jason's smiling photo looking up at me.

"Oh, Jason," I say out loud as I pick up the paper and almost reverently place it on the coffee table with his picture facing up, "why did you do this?"

I stand up and wander into the kitchen now. I'm not hungry, but my stomach is aching like I consumed a bowlful of rusty nails and battery acid, and I wonder if there's something I can eat that will make it stop hurting. I open the fridge and look inside, but the smell of the food makes me want to hurl. I shut the door and turn away.

I go into the bathroom now. It's one that my mom and I share since our house was built in an era when people thought one bath-room was sufficient for the entire family. I open the old-fashioned medicine cabinet thinking I will take a big gulp of that disgusting Pepto-Bismol stuff, but the pink bottle is nearly empty, and even when I turn it upside down and shake it hard, I can get only a few drops on my tongue. I throw it into the wastebasket and look back in the medicine cabinet.

My head is throbbing like it will never stop. So I reach for the extra-strength Advil that I normally use for cramps, but then I notice a red-and-white bottle of Tylenol sitting right next to it. And then, as if I'm compelled by an outside force, I pick up the bottle of Tylenol instead. I give it a shake and can tell that it's almost full. Then I open it up and look at those innocent-looking white pills and wonder, *Can this stuff really kill you?*

Oh, I've heard of kids taking pills before. Like Penny Weitzig, when we were just freshmen. She took a whole bottle of something and then got scared and called 911 and was taken to the ER, where she got her stomach pumped. We all felt sorry for her and everyone was extra nice to her when she came back to school. At least for a couple of days.

My head feels like it's going to burst, so I pop two Tylenol pills into my mouth, then lean over the sink and wash them down with some foul-tasting lukewarm water.

But instead of returning the bottle of Tylenol to the medicine cabinet, I take it back into the living room with me and set it on the coffee table right next to the newspaper. I have no idea why I'm doing this, but there's this driving force, something that's compelling me. Maybe it's Jason.

But now my stomach is really starting to hurt and I realize that I haven't eaten anything all day and it's after four now, so I force myself to drink half a glass of milk. Then I go back into the living room and sit on the couch and stare blankly at the large oak coffee table with the newspaper and Tylenol sitting on it. Then I go and gather several candles from around the house, as well as matches. And I place these on the coffee table too.

Then I go into my bedroom and search out everything that has anything to do with Jason, and I bring these items out to the living room and neatly arrange them on the coffee table with the rest of what is becoming a little shrine. There's the CD Jason gave me for my last birthday, the worn baseball mitt he gave me when he outgrew it, several photos of him that I've taken over the years, starting from when I first got interested in photography in middle school up to the ones I took just a couple of weeks ago—even an old yellow T-shirt of his that had shrunk and I'd scavenged. It says "SoccerKidz" on the pocket.

Then I light the candles and sit down on the couch and just stare at my strange creation. The candles grow blurry as my eyes once again fill with tears. And I keep asking myself, *Why, why, why?*

For the first time today, I consider praying. Prayer used to get me through some pretty tough times. But the truth is, I haven't been praying at all during the past month. I've quit reading my Bible and going to youth group too. At first I told myself that I was just "taking a break." But honestly, I was mad at God. It seemed to me that no matter how hard I tried, my life never seemed to get much better. And then this whole thing with Mom and Bradley just kept getting more and more out of control. And I guess I just decided that God had quit listening to me anyway.

So now there's this huge obstacle—I'm not even sure what it is—but it's like a giant wall between God and me, and even if I wanted to—which I don't, especially in light of what's happened today—I'm not sure how I'd get over it.

In fact, that wall seems to be growing bigger and wider by the minute. Maybe it's actually a mountain. But I think if I were going to say anything to God right now, I could only yell and scream at him and demand to know why he let something like this happen to Jason. But the fact is, I am not talking to God right now. I may never speak to him again.

Still, I want to talk to someone. I wish my mom were here, and I hate Bradley even more for taking her away right when I need her the most.

I start pacing in the living room. I feel like a trapped animal, like I want to claw down the walls and tear up the furniture. I think I might go crazy if I stay in this house one minute longer. So I blow out the candles, shove my feet into my flip-flops, and go outside.

It seems all wrong that the sun is shining and the trees are blossoming and all kinds of spring flowers are in bloom. How dare they look so cheerful and carefree when my whole world is black and hopeless?

My feet know exactly where they are going, and I let them lead me up Tamarack Street. I know I am heading directly toward his house, and I have no idea why I am doing this, but it's like I can't stop myself. The Hardings' house is only a few blocks from mine, but these two neighborhoods couldn't be more different. Both are part of the old section of town, where most of the houses are fifty years old and older, but my house is located at the foot of the hill, whereas Jason's is halfway up and has a nice view of the city and river. And there you have it, the difference between the haves and the have-nots.

I feel slightly breathless when I reach the place where Pine Street intersects Tamarack. I pause before I turn left and continue walking. All the houses up here are familiar to me since I've been coming up here for years. But today I don't even see them. It's as if I am walking with my eyes closed.

I make sure to keep my distance from the Harding house by walking on the other side of the street. I'm not even sure why I do this, but I think it may be to show respect. I don't want his family to think I'm being weird. Finally I stop and, leaning against the rock retaining wall on the house behind me, I just stare at Jason's house. I can see his bedroom window from here. The shades are drawn.

In fact, all the curtains and shades seem to be down in the Harding house. It's as if the entire house has retreated into itself in mourning. I see Mr. Harding's Toyota Land Cruiser in the driveway and suspect that Mrs. Harding's Honda Accord is in the garage. Maybe that's where Jason's car is too. Although he usually parks it out on the street. He said he liked how out of place his beat-up '83 Buick Century looked on their pristine lane, where homeowners are looked down on if they leave their trash cans on the curb too long. His dad, a successful Realtor, as well as a city councilman, was always trying to get Jason to park his "hunk-a-junk," as he called it, in the garage so the neighbors wouldn't be offended. Well, I guess they won't be offended anymore.

"My dad's pretty uptight," Jason told me a couple of weeks ago, and I sensed he was discouraged. "He's really into appearances."

"Probably because of his work," I'd offered, as if I really knew anything about it.

"Yeah, maybe."

I knew that Jason didn't really like to criticize his parents, but something was bugging him. Even so, I cringe to remember my off-hand comment that day: "Hey, you're lucky," I said to him. "My mom couldn't care less about appearances right now. I mean, she goes tripping around like she's fifteen. Talk about embarrassing."

And that's all it took to shift the conversation back to one of our favorite topics—Morgan Bergstrom and her messed-up family. I could always make Jason look good.

I look back up at his picture-perfect house and take in a long, slow breath. More than anything right now, I wish it was possible to speak to the dead. There's so much I need to know.

five

"HEY," A GUY'S VOICE CALLS FROM BEHIND ME. I NEARLY JUMP OUT OF MY flip-flops. But suddenly I'm thinking it's him—it's Jason and he really is alive and this whole thing is really just a big, bad joke. I turn around with hopeful eyes only to see Seth Blum sauntering across the yard toward me.

"Morgan," he says, "I thought that was you."

"Hey," I say, my voice flat with disappointment.

Seth, as usual, is wearing his personal uniform of a black T-shirt and black cargo pants. I think it's his statement against the world. Today's T-shirt has a Nine Inch Nails logo across the chest. Not very cheerful, but kind of fitting.

"It's hard to believe," he says as he sits on the rock wall.

I nod as I lean against the wall again, looking back across the street. "I don't even know why I came up here . . ." I start to choke up.

Seth puts his hand on my shoulder. "We're all hurting, Morgan. I couldn't even go to school today. It's just too hard."

I turn and look at Seth. As far as I know, he and Jason haven't been close friends since middle school, but they've known each other forever. And I know that Seth, never quite as popular as his well-liked neighbor, still looked up to Jason. Of course, Jason had always been nice to Seth and even gave him assignments for the newspaper, despite Seth's gloomy perspective about life in general. That's just the kind of guy Jason is. Was.

"I didn't even know it had happened until after first period," I admit to Seth as I wipe my dripping nose on the sleeve of my sweatshirt. "And then I just totally lost it."

He nods. "Yeah, that's why I stayed home."

"They sent me home."

There's this long pause, and we both just stare pathetically at the sad-looking house across the street.

"I just don't get it," I finally say.

"Me neither." He runs his hand through his long hair. "Well, maybe I do, sort of."

"Sort of?"

"Not for Jason. I mean, I sort of understand it for myself."

"Huh?" I turn and look at him.

"Like out of everyone I know, Jason had it all. He had everything going for him."

"I know." I sigh and wish once again that this was all just a bad dream.

"It doesn't make much sense." Then he turns and looks at me. "You were good friends with him, Morgan. Did he say anything to give you any kind of clue, anything to make you know that he was hurting enough to do something like this?"

I consider the question but don't answer. Maybe he did. Suddenly I'm thinking that Jason might've been giving me all sorts of clues, but maybe I was just too self-absorbed to listen. I mean, I was the one who was always complaining to him about my pathetic little life. Compared to mine, his seemed like a walk in the park. And I even said that to him, more times than I'd like to admit.

"I know he was worried about his GPA," I finally say. "He said he had to bring his spring term grades up if he was going to get into Princeton. You know his dad was really pushing for that. It was a big deal to him to have all three kids graduate from Princeton."

"Jason was always trying to keep up with Aaron and Jessica," says Seth.

"Pretty hard acts to follow, don't you think?"

"Yeah." He just shakes his head.

"It's not like Jason expected to get scholarships like they did. He just wanted to get in. That's all."

"Man," says Seth. "I'd be happy just to get into MSU." Then he lets loose with a cuss word.

"I feel so lost without him," I say. "I just don't know what to do."

"I know."

The tears are coming again. "And I miss him so much. It's so — so wrong."

Then Seth puts his arms around me and holds me in a long hug while I just sob until his T-shirt and Nine Inch Nails are all wet.

"I'm sorry," I say as I step back. "I got you all soggy."

"It's okay." He has tears streaming down his face too, trickling like tiny streams through his unshaved stubble and dripping down his chin. "I feel lost too, Morgan. Like if someone as together as Jason Harding can't make it . . ." He sighs and pushes his shaggy hair away from his face. "Man, how can a freak like me possibly survive?"

"You're not a freak," I begin, but I know that most of the kids at SHS wouldn't agree. "You're just very unique, that's all."

He looks unconvinced as he sadly shakes his head. "I'm scared, Morgan."

"Scared?" I echo, although to be perfectly honest, I feel scared too. In fact, that's exactly how I feel. Like this thing with Jason has totally rocked me and it will never be right again. Even so, it makes no sense. Nothing makes sense.

"Yeah. Like I'm thinking if it's that easy to check out, and life is so messed up, well, why not just get it over with? You know what I mean?"

I don't say anything. But the fact is, I *do* know. And even weirder than that is how I don't completely disagree with him. I'm just not sure I could do something like that. I guess I'm not sure of anything anymore.

six

"ISN'T THAT GRACE BENSON'S CAR?" SETH SAYS SUDDENLY. HE'S POINTING to a red Geo that's creeping up the street toward us.

Jason dated Grace, off and on, for the past year or so. And I know he really liked her, but it seemed like one thing or another was always pulling them apart. As she gets closer, I hold up my hand in a feeble wave, and she pulls over and parks her car on the street next to us.

Now, it's not that I don't like her, but Grace and I have never been very close. Mostly, I think, because she's been jealous of my friendship with Jason. In fact, I'm sure that had to do with why she broke up with him this last time, shortly after Christmas. She just couldn't accept that he and I could possibly be nothing more than good friends, although we both tried to reassure her of this fact.

Even behind her dark glasses, it's easy to see that Grace is beautiful. Not only is she tall and willowy, but with her thick dark hair and olive-toned skin, she looks like someone you'd see on a fashion runway. I suppose in some ways I have always been a little jealous of her too.

Of course, her life hasn't been exactly easy. Being "racially mixed" has had its challenges for Grace. Jason has told me lots of sad stories about things that have happened when she's been out with her parents and some stupid racist stranger has gotten mouthy and said something totally lame.

"Hey, Morgan . . . Seth," she says in husky voice that tells me that she has been crying too.

Before we can say anything else, we are all sobbing and hugging each other tightly, right there in the middle of the sidewalk. The three of us are in this close circle, just hanging onto each other as if we are all long-lost friends instead of casual acquaintances suddenly linked together by loss.

We finally disentangle and look blankly across the street at Jason's house. I'm sure that anyone watching us right now, if they didn't know what was going on, would think we were the most lost-looking threesome in the world.

"I skipped school after I heard the news on the radio this morning," she says as she reaches in her jeans pocket for a rumpled tissue to wipe her nose. "I knew I'd be a mess if I went. But after sitting around the house all day, I was just getting more and more depressed. I guess I thought it might help to come up here and just see his house, you know, the last place he . . ." She shakes her head and chokes back another sob. "But it's not helping. It's just making me feel worse."

"I know what you mean," I admit. "It's like the pain doesn't ease up. It just seems to intensify."

"*Why did he do it?*" Her voice is angry now. "Why, of all people, did Jason Harding do something like this?"

"We were wondering the same thing," says Seth.

"He had it all!" says Grace. "Brains, looks, money. Why did he just throw it away like that?"

"And us," I add in a mousy voice. "He threw us away too."

Seth cusses and pulls a pack of cigarettes out of one of his deep cargo pockets. He offers me one, but I just shake my head. To my surprise, Grace accepts. And Seth uses his shiny black Zippo to light it for her.

"It just makes me feel like giving up," she says as she blows out a fierce stream of smoke. "I mean, why should we bother with this freaking life if someone like Jason Harding couldn't handle it?"

"That's just what I was saying to Morgan," says Seth. It sounds vaguely familiar, but I don't recall him saying those exact words.

Suddenly the two of them are really into this idea, acting as if they seriously want to take their own lives. I'm sure it's just talk and I don't know that I even care anyway. I let their words float over my head with their cigarette smoke. All I can think about right now is Jason—and how much I love him, and how much I already miss him, and how I will never see him again. Man, it just hurts so bad.

"What do you think, Morgan?" asks Grace.

"Think?" I frown at her. "About what?"

"About Seth's idea?"

"I guess I wasn't listening. I think I was kinda spacing . . . just thinking about Jason, you know?"

"Yeah, I know." She nods as she drops her cigarette butt and grinds it down with the heel of her sandal. "But Seth and I were just making a little escape plan for ourselves and we thought you might be interested."

"Yeah," says Seth, and I can see that his eyes look slightly hopeful now, almost as if something has changed. "We could be with him, you know."

"*With* him?" I query.

"Yeah," says Grace. "We could join him."

"Do you even know *where* he is?" I ask.

"Jason believed in God," says Grace. "He told me so enough times. Maybe he's in heaven."

"Oh, I'm not so sure . . ." I begin.

"Nobody's sure of anything," says Grace quickly.

"Except that life sucks," adds Seth. "Thousands of innocent children are dying from AIDS in Africa. The Middle East is determined to destroy themselves and us too. Chemicals in the environment are poisoning everyone. Really, what is there to live for?"

I really don't have an answer for that, so I just sigh and look at Jason's bedroom window.

"I wish there was someplace we could go," says Grace, looking over her shoulder. "I feel so conspicuous here."

"We could go to my house," says Seth. "Except that my mom's there now."

"No one's home at my house," I offer, then wonder why I did.

But I have no chance to take it back as we pile into Grace's tiny car and she drives us down the hill toward my house.

I don't even bother to apologize for my unimpressive and slightly messy house as I take them both inside. Who really cares anyway? And once inside they are both mesmerized by my coffee table shrine, which makes me very uncomfortable. Why did I even let them in here?

"It's silly, I know," I begin.

"No," says Grace as she sits down on the couch. "It's kind of cool."

Seth sits down beside her and I just stand there feeling as if I am naked.

"Can we light the candles?" asks Grace. She's already holding the matches.

"Sure," I tell her as I sit down in the chair across from them.

Seth picks up my bottle of Tylenol and looks at me suspiciously. "Were you thinking of—"

"I had a headache," I quickly tell him.

He looks unconvinced.

Grace picks up a photo of Jason and just stares. It's one that I took recently, and it's really pretty good. It's black and white and he's looking off to one side with a really thoughtful, faraway look. He didn't even know I was taking it at the time.

"This is good," she tells me.

"Thanks."

"Are you going to keep this up?" she asks. "Like go into it professionally?"

I just shrug. "I've heard it's pretty hard to make a living at photography."

"He was really good-looking, wasn't he?" she says in a wistful voice.

"Yeah, he was," I agree.

Then she looks back up at me. "Did you love him too?"

"Of course I loved him, Grace. He was one of my closest friends. But was I in love with him? Are you asking me if I was in love with him?"

"Yeah, I guess so."

"No," I tell her. "I was not in love with Jason. We tried dating once, but it just ruined everything. We were a lot better off just being friends."

She looks truly surprised. "Really?"

"Honestly. Just friends. But very good friends."

"So I guess I shouldn't have gotten so bent out of shape over you, huh?"

"Guess not." I lean back in my chair now and close my eyes. "I miss him so much."

And then we all begin to talk about him. We share little things that no one else knows. It's almost as if we're having our own private memorial service for him.

"Hey," says Seth. "It's almost time for the six o'clock news. Should we see if they know anything else? Like if they've found a note or why he did it?"

Before he's even finished, I have the TV turned on and tuned to the local news station. We all wait quietly as that stupid commercial about toenail fungus rattles on and on, and finally we see Mike Thompson from Channel 5 News saying hello and today's date. After reporting on a local fire that killed an elderly man and a pro-life protest in front of a downtown abortion clinic, he finally comes to the topic we've been waiting for.

"Teen suicide rates are on the increase across the country, and recently the epidemic hit close to home. Surviving friends and relatives of eighteen-year-old Jason Harding are saddened and confused by what seems a senseless loss of life. In the early hours of the morning, Harding succumbed to liver failure after ingesting what is estimated to have been between eighty and ninety Tylenol tablets. We spoke to some of the bereaved today."

Then the screen changes to Coach Spangler, and the reporter is asking about Jason.

"He was a good kid," says our basketball coach. "You couldn't ask for a better team player out on the court." He sadly shakes his head. "All the kids in that family have been a real blessing to this school. And they're all in our prayers now."

Next we see Chelsea Summers' tear-streaked face. Grace lets out a painful moan. "What's she doing on there?"

Chelsea is a somewhat superficial cheerleader-type chick and not even a close friend of Jason's, but she can usually be found at the center of any opportunity for attention. "We all miss Jason sooo much," she says into the camera. "He was like the sweetest guy ever. And no one can figure it out, like why he did something like this . . ." She breaks up. "We just—we just wish he was still here with us."

Then it's Marcus Nickerson's face on the TV. Surprised to see our youth pastor, I lean forward to listen. "We all loved Jason," he says in a somber voice. "We don't know why this happened and we're all very upset with the news. But we're praying for his family and trusting God to bring good out of bad."

A final comment from Mike Thompson, and then they switch to sports and I turn it off.

"Who was that last guy?" asks Seth.

"The youth pastor at Eastside," I say as I set down the remote.

"So no one really knows what was wrong," says Grace.

"Maybe Jason was just fed up and wanted out." Seth leans back and sighs. "Can't say that I blame him."

"It's so unreal,". says Grace. "I keep trying to imagine where he is right now. How he feels. Whether it's better."

"Why don't we find out?" Seth raises his eyebrows and my Tylenol bottle simultaneously.

"Are you really serious?" I ask.

He nods. "Yeah, I'm pretty sure that I'm going to do it. And anyone who wants to join me is welcome." He looks hopefully at Grace. "I mean, who knows what we'll find on the other side. Maybe if we hurry up we'll get there about the same time as Jason."

Grace is nodding, like she's really buying into this. "I'm open," she says. "But I guess I want to think about it first. I mean, it's a pretty big decision."

"We're all going to die eventually," says Seth. "So why should we go on being tortured like this? Why not just hurry things along?"

Grace looks at her watch and jumps up. "Shoot. I've gotta go. You need a ride, Seth?"

"Yeah, I guess."

"You going to be okay on your own, Morgan?" asks Grace with what seems like genuine concern. "Like, when's your mom getting back?"

"Sunday."

She frowns. "I don't think I could handle being alone right now."

I shrug. "That's life, huh?"

"Doesn't have to be that way," says Seth as he puts a hand on my shoulder.

I glance at him, unsure of his meaning.

"We should stick together," he says. "I think that's what Jason would want. Don't you?"

"Yeah, maybe," says Grace. "It's kind of like he's brought us together or something."

"I think he really wants us to join him," says Seth. "I've got this feeling deep inside of me, like it's the right thing to do, you know?"

Though Seth seems totally sincere and is also somewhat convincing, I'm still not too sure.

"Maybe we could do it here, Morgan," he says suddenly as he glances around my house. "I mean, if we all decide to do it together. It would be better to do it someplace where no one's home. So it doesn't get botched up, you know." He looks hopefully at me. "What do you think?"

"I think I need to think about this," I tell him, wondering what there is to think about. His idea is pretty out there. Well, mostly anyway.

seven

SOON THEY ARE GONE AND MY HOUSE FEELS MORE EMPTY AND LONELY than ever. I just walk around and around, wishing that the aching inside me would go away, or even just let up a little. How does a person go on living with this kind of never-ending pain? That alone should be enough to kill you.

Maybe Seth is right. Maybe it would be a relief.

I walk around in a kind of daze, looking at everything in my house as if I'm seeing it for the first (or is it the last?) time, because despite myself, I am beginning to consider Seth's "escape plan." What is there about my life that should give me a reason to keep going? Especially now that Jason is gone? And in just two days my mom is going to come back here with my new stepdad. How much fun will that be?

I can just see us now, *the happy family*. Toss my messed-up brother back into the picture if he ever decides to come home, and we could try to get on one of those reality shows where people win money for driving each other crazy. It occurs to me that I haven't seen Jonathan in more than a week now. As much as his lifestyle totally bugs me, I still worry about him. For all I know, he could be dead too. I've heard that deaths from drug overdoses are on the rise in our community.

Really, I am asking myself, what *is* there to live for? I mean, wouldn't it be worth it to end this pain?

Just then the phone rings and I practically jump out of my skin. I go to the phone in the kitchen, the one with caller ID, and wait to see who it is. To my surprise it says Marcus Nickerson. Even so, I don't pick up. Don't ask me why, but I just don't think I can bear to talk to a youth pastor right now, especially since I haven't been to youth group in weeks. I listen as the machine takes it, then wait to see if Marcus will leave a message.

"Hi, Morgan," says a female voice that I recognize as Marcus' wife. "This is Tracie. I've really been thinking about you and praying for you today. I'm sure you must be hurting pretty badly right now. We all are. In fact, a bunch of us are getting together here at the church. Carlie says to say hi. Anyway, we'd love to have you come join us. Or if you need anyone to talk to, please, feel free to call me. Anytime, Morgan, even if it's late. Okay? Really, I'm here for you. And, hey, I've missed you at youth group lately. So just call, okay?"

Then she hangs up and I feel guilty for not picking up. Tracie was one of the first people in youth group, besides Jason, who was actually friendly to me. And she always looks so happy when she sees me and she notices every time that I'm not there.

"I am such a jerk," I say out loud. What is wrong with me that I can't even answer the stupid phone? What kind of lame excuse for a friend am I?

I go back into the kitchen and pick up the phone, deciding to just call her, but something stops me. As I'm thinking about what a rotten friend I am, I remember something from an e-mail Jason sent earlier this week. I remember how he had sounded pretty down. And I remember how I'd been really busy researching my history paper, and I'm not even sure if I took the time to e-mail him back. I am such a jerk!

I go to my room and turn on my computer and impatiently wait to get online. Then I go straight to my e-mail thinking I'll pull up his last message. I can't even remember what he said. To my surprise there is a new message from him, dated yesterday at 4:40 PM. The subject line is blank.

I take a deep breath and hold it, double click on his name, then wait for his message to open. I read his words and feel like someone has just slugged me in the stomach.

You there, Morgan? Just want to talk to someone. Feeling down. Can't get up. So tired. J

That's all. I read those five lines over and over, trying to see if I missed something. My guess is that he'd already taken the Tylenol by the time he wrote this and maybe he was about to doze off. But he said he wanted to talk. I wonder what he wanted to say. More than that, I wonder why I hadn't gone online and checked my e-mail yesterday. Maybe I could've done something to stop this whole thing. But I didn't. When Jason really needed a friend—needed me—I wasn't there for him. I make myself sick!

And that's all it takes. Now I am sobbing again, only more hysterically now. I am absolutely certain that it's my fault Jason is dead. If only I'd been a better friend, he might be alive right now. If only I hadn't been so self-absorbed and pathetic.

But as usual, I was obsessing over my own stupid life, freaking out over something as insignificant as my mom's plans to marry Bradley. Meanwhile, one of my best friends was so down that he was taking his own life.

I go back into the living room, where the candles are still burning. Sitting down on the couch, I just stare at his photos. I look into his eyes and know that I could have prevented this. If only I'd been available.

I pick up the bottle of Tylenol and open it, shaking a handful of pills into my hand. Michael Thompson on Channel 5 News said that Jason took eighty to ninety pills. I wonder how many are here. I read the contents on the bottle's label to see that it originally held eighty and it looks to be mostly full now. And since I weigh quite a bit less than Jason, I think that it's probably sufficient to do the deed.

Still, I feel scared. Questions that I am unwilling to acknowledge are mumbling inside my brain. I'm not sure I can actually do this. But how can I not? How can I possibly go on?

Then I remember Seth and Grace, and I think that this really might be easier to do with someone else. Less frightening at least.

I carefully pour the pills back into their bottle, replace the child-proof cap, and put it into my sweatshirt pocket for safekeeping. It's like these pills suddenly seem very precious to me. I am slightly amazed at how open I have become to actually killing myself.

I almost think I could do it right now. Right here. By myself. No one would even discover my body until Sunday. And I even feel a vague sense of satisfaction thinking that my mom and Bradley would come home to something like this. Because, really, Jason's death is partly their fault. If I hadn't been so distracted by their insanity, I might've thought to go online and check my e-mail and maybe I would've been able to stop Jason. Who knows? Anyway, they should suffer some too.

I decide to call Seth. I find his number in the phone book and when he answers I tell him about the e-mail and how bummed I am. Then I tell him that *I am in.*

"That's cool," he says calmly. "When do you want to do it?"

"Tomorrow evening. How about you come around five?" I

answer as if we're just planning to meet at Starbucks for coffee. "But I only have enough Tylenol for one. You'll have to bring your own."

To my surprise this makes him laugh. "It's a BYOT party," he says.

"Huh?"

"You know, Bring Your Own Tylenol."

"Right," I answer in a flat voice.

"I'll let Grace know," he tells me before we both hang up.

And it's weird, because after I set the phone down, after I know it's all settled, I almost begin to feel better. Like maybe checking out really is the best answer. It's like I've suddenly gotten control over my life again. And who knows where this might take us? Maybe Seth is right, maybe we'll be with Jason before long.

The phone rings again around seven. I check the caller ID to see that it's the Nickersons again. I wait and listen as Tracie makes yet another plea for me to call her. But I do not pick up. She is probably the last person I want to talk to right now. It's not that I don't like her. I do. But she's extremely perceptive, at least with me. She might suspect something's wrong, maybe even figure out about our little suicide pact. And I'm certain that she and Marcus would do everything possible to stop us.

I try to remember exactly what made me quit going to youth group or, more accurately, turn my back on God. I guess it was a series of things really. I tried to explain it to Jason only a couple of weeks ago. I think it was shortly after my mom had started sleeping with Bradley—in our house—and I was feeling very angry about life in general.

"This whole God thing is just not working for me," I told Jason the day he asked me if I needed a ride to youth group. "It's like the more I pray and read my Bible and the harder I try to live my life right, the worse things get."

"Yeah," he agreed. "I know how you feel."

"I mean, it's like God isn't even listening to me, like he's not even there."

"But he is," said Jason.

"Maybe for you."

"Hey, my life's not going any better than yours."

Now it hurts to remember this, but I actually got mad at him for saying that. "Yeah, you bet," I said in my most sarcastic tone. "Your life is so freaking bad, Jason. You've got two totally functional parents who really care about you. You live in a great house. Everyone at school likes you. How can you even compare your life to mine?"

Then I went on, in great detail, to remind him of my drug-addict brother, my midlife-crisis mother and her dippy boyfriend, who spends more nights at our house than his own, and my dead-beat dad, who pays child support when he's in the mood and then just vanishes when he's not.

"And don't even get me started on our pathetic finances," I finish. "Unless I get a scholarship, which is looking pretty iffy right now, I probably won't even get to go to a real college."

"Okay, okay." He held his hands up as if to surrender. "You win, Morgan. As always, your life sucks way worse than mine."

"And so," I told him, "I have decided that if this is how crappy things get when I'm trying to live my life for God, well, maybe I should see if it gets any better without him."

He kind of laughed then. "Well, keep me posted."

"But you don't need to tell anyone," I said, not sure I wanted my friends at youth group to get all freaked out over my spiritual condition and start praying for me or calling me or whatever. "Who knows? I might change my mind in a day or two."

But I didn't. And not because my life got any better either. The truth is, it has only gotten worse. Much, much worse. Still, I'm sure it was heading in this direction anyway. So I stuck my Bible in a drawer, and with each passing day it got easier and easier to just ignore God. And after a week, when Jason invited me to youth group again, I told him I'd pass.

"So how's it working for you?" he asked. "You still off of God?"

"Yep."

"And you're okay with that?"

"I guess."

"Don't you miss him?" asked Jason.

Okay, the truth was I actually did miss God. But for some reason I couldn't admit this to Jason. I told him that my life was just as sucky now as it had been before.

"God just doesn't make any difference," I said. "If anything, God is a setup for me to expect that things are going to change and get better. And then they just keep getting worse. So why bother?"

By then I had noticed how some of my Christian friends were treating me like I had some kind of a fungus disease, or like I was the enemy, or the rebellious Christian, or whatever. But they were obviously avoiding me. Even Carlie, who'd been my best friend, was acting like I was a bad influence or something. But Jason was never like that. No one has ever been as good a friend or as loyal as Jason. I can't believe he's gone. And I can't believe how much I took him for granted. I never deserved him.

eight

THE PHONE RINGS AGAIN AROUND EIGHT. I CHECK THE CALLER ID AND SEE that it's Carlie this time. I'm not sure whether to pick up or not. Finally I do.

"Hey, you're there," she says. "How's it going?"

"Not too well."

"I know. This is so sad."

"Tell me about it."

"We were really hoping you'd show up at church this evening. There were lots of kids there. And not just youth group kids either. It was actually pretty cool."

"*Pretty cool?*" I echo. "Like you guys were having a party or something? Celebrating the fact that—"

"No, no. It wasn't like that, not at all. We were just trying to comfort each other, you know. Kids were talking about Jason and asking questions about life and God and—"

"Well, that's really nice, Carlie. But I should probably get off the phone in case my mom tries to call."

"Okay, but if you need to talk, Morgan, I'm—"

"Yeah, I know," I cut her off again. "You're there for me, right?"

"Right."

"Thanks. See ya."

"Take care."

And then I hang up. Okay, it does occur to me that this could be the last time I speak to Carlie, ever, but then maybe it's for the best. Maybe Carlie and the rest of the so-called Christians will feel bad for the way they've treated me these past few weeks—acting like I was the one with the problem. Maybe this will be a real wake-up call for everyone. Maybe that's what Jason had in mind.

The phone rings again and I feel myself getting fed up with all these stupid phone calls. Can't people just leave me alone? Then I wonder if it might actually be my mom calling this time. And to my surprise, I am sprinting to the kitchen, really hoping that it's her. But I discover it's Grace. Curious as to what she wants, I pick up.

"Hey," I say in a sad tone.

"How's it going?" she asks in an equally sad tone.

"It's been better."

"Yeah. I know."

"Did Seth call you?" I ask.

"Yeah. He says you're going to do it."

"Uh-huh. I thought about it and I honestly don't think I can go on, you know. I just don't want to live in this messed-up world anymore."

"Yeah, me neither."

"So are you in too?"

"Yeah. At least I am right now. I guess I'm still a little nervous. I mean, it's pretty weird to think about, you know. But I just talked with Seth for a long time and I feel pretty sure that it's the right thing to do. And like he says, we'll be with Jason soon, and we'll all be together forever."

"I told Seth we should meet around five o'clock tomorrow," I say. "Not that we'll do it right then. I think maybe we should do it later, you know, like maybe during the night. I'm not really sure . . . but you guys can come over around then. Maybe we can talk some more first."

Grace says that sounds cool and then we both hang up. I'm not totally sure she's going to go through with this thing. For that matter, I'm not totally sure that I will either. Oh, it's not that I don't want to do it. I mean, I really do want to check out—I seriously do. I'm so tired of feeling this bummed. And I don't see how anything will ever get any better for me. But I guess I'm just worried that I might chicken out by tomorrow.

For the first time today, I notice that the red light on the answering machine is flashing and I guess maybe I should check the messages, just in case. Mostly I want to see if my mom called while I was gone. For some reason I think that could make a difference, but I don't even know why.

So I hit the play button and then quickly flip through several messages only to discover that most are from some stupid roofing company that thinks we want a new roof. There's also one from Carlie calling from school earlier today to check on me, and then to my surprise there's a message from my grandma. As usual, she drones on and on about almost nothing—talking about how some kind of cactus flower is blooming in some desert out West. As if I care. Then she says something about coming for a visit and how she feels concerned about Mom. Well, she should be!

As I hit the Skip button, I wonder what on earth is wrong with my family? I mean, why is everyone so flaky? There was a time when I thought Grandma really cared about us. She helped us out after my dad left and even let us live in her house with her. Then it's like she had some kind of meltdown. She hooked up with this old dude from California—the kind of guy who wears heavy gold chains and looks like he spent too much time in the sun. She thought he was her soul mate, so she bought herself a motor home and took off with him on some kind of I-gotta-see-the-world-before-I-die quest. Fortunately for her (at least in my opinion anyway) the old dude split after a few months, but my grandma is still out there rambling around the West in her Winnebago. Pretty weird if you ask me.

I decide to delete all of the messages. I hit the button again and again. Delete. Delete. Delete. Maybe it's this easy to delete an entire life. Like, here today, gone tomorrow. In a morbid way I find this concept rather fascinating. I mean, to think you can be alive and well today and then totally dead tomorrow. Just like that. But in another way I guess it's pretty scary. I can't imagine what it feels like to not be here. What happens? Do you just cease to exist? Or is there an afterlife? And what about God and heaven? Ugh. I don't really want to think about that now. If I think about that tonight, I might just fall apart completely.

And so I try to blot out all my thoughts as I rattle around in the house by myself. I play loud music, the kind that sort of empties your head, and I try to pretend like I'm not even here. Like I don't really exist, like I'm already gone.

But it's not really working and I finally give up and just sit down in the darkened living room. I don't remember ever feeling as lonely as I feel tonight. And I keep reaching into my sweatshirt pocket for my Tylenol bottle, my little security blanket. And the lonelier I feel, the more certain I become. More and more, I feel convinced that I will go through with this thing tomorrow. Because I do *not* want to keep living like this. If you could even call this living. No one should have to go through life like this. It's just not worth the energy. Or the pain. I'm really sick of the pain.

Finally it's midnight and although I'm exhausted, I'm afraid to turn off the lights and go to bed. I know that it's silly and that I'm acting pretty neurotic, but I just can't help myself. I feel certain that I'm not going to be able to sleep at all. And I can't stand the idea of lying in my bed with all the lights off, just being wide awake and thinking about Jason—and where he is and what has happened to him. The gaping hole in my chest just keeps getting bigger and bigger.

I go back to the medicine cabinet, hoping that my mom might have some kind of over-the-counter sleeping pills, although I've never noticed her using anything like that before. But there are none to be found. I go into her bedroom and snoop around, hoping that maybe I'll find something in there. I mean, don't all adults use sleeping pills occasionally?

I am pleasantly surprised to find a brand-new bottle of vodka in her underwear drawer. Bingo! Maybe I can have a few drinks just to help me relax. Now, I've never been into drinking, mostly because I was too busy being a good little Christian. Even during my "rebellious" period of the past several weeks, it had never occurred to me to start drinking. Well, I'm thinking it's not too late to try it now.

I take the bottle into the kitchen and wonder what I should mix it with. Somehow I don't think I'm ready to drink this stuff straight up. I decide on orange juice, which I think might actually make some kind of a drink. So I fill a third of a glass with vodka, then add an equal amount of juice and take a sip. It tastes kind of like orange juice that's gone bad, but I find that if I chug it down quickly enough, it's not so bad.

I go into the living room and turn on the TV, searching for a movie that might help put me to sleep. But the movie I select only makes me feel more wide-awake than ever, and so I head back to the kitchen and make myself another drink. A full glass this time.

Apparently that does the trick, because when I wake up quite early the next morning and still on the couch, it feels like a dead horse has been sleeping in my mouth all night, and my head is pounding like the SHS marching band on an off-key day. In fact, I feel so crappy that it takes me a while to remember exactly how I got into this condition in the first place. But that's when I notice my coffee table shrine, and I am reminded. I pick up my favorite photo of Jason and just stare into his eyes. I never realized that he had such nice eyes. But those eyes can't see anymore. They are closed. Closed forever.

I take in a shaky breath and remind myself that today is *the* day. I set the photo with the others and it occurs to me that I should make sure that Jason's parents get these photos of him after I'm gone. Maybe I can write that in my note. Because, unlike Jason, I definitely plan on leaving a note.

This is my last day to live, I remind myself as I stand up unsteadily and look around the messy living room. And maybe I should get busy. But what do you do when you know that it's your last day to be alive? And how can I do anything with this throbbing in my head? I take just two Tylenol to ease this temporary pain and save the rest for tonight when I'll put an end to all of my pain forever.

To my surprise I actually feel like eating today. Not just eating either, it's like I'm ravenous. First I have a bowl of corn flakes, then I make scrambled eggs with swiss cheese. Then I make some chocolate milk and open a bag of cheese puffs and start scarfing those down.

I worry for about two seconds that I'm going to get fat if I keep pigging out like this, but then I remember that I won't have time to get fat. I will be dead.

I take a shower and put on my favorite outfit, which really isn't so special since it's just my best jeans, a graphic tee, and the jean jacket I talked my mom into getting me for Christmas. Since it's sunny outside I decide to wear my flip-flops again. Then I get my camera and every roll of film I have (the sixteen rolls that Jason gave me last week—film that was meant to be used for the yearbook) and I put these into my backpack and head outside.

First I walk to the school and get my bike. Then I take off riding. I ride all over town and I shoot pictures of everything, from dented lampposts to kids in the park to a grisly old man waiting for the downtown bus. I love the feel of my old Nikon 35 mm in my hands, like an old friend. Mr. Spencer makes me use the digital camera at school sometimes, but I don't think the photo quality compares with these old guys. And I don't mind getting my film loaded onto disks. I think it's worth the effort.

As I take all these random pictures, I feel like I'm seeing my town through a different set of eyes. Maybe it's the artist in me, or maybe I'm just documenting the last day of my life. I even find myself daydreaming that someone will discover my rolls of film, get them developed, and turn all these cool photos into a book that could be titled *The Last Day of My Life*. And then I could become posthumously famous and maybe my mom could even get rich from the book sales and she could retire and move to Florida with dear, sweet Bradley.

Well, who knows?

For a few brief moments I almost imagine that I am having fun. But then, almost as if someone has dropped a bucket of ice water over my head, *I remember Jason*—and everything looks bleak and hopeless again. And I wonder how I could've been so deceived, if only for a moment.

I pause for lunch, since I am once again ravenous, and remembering that I am no longer counting calories or eating low-carb, I go to Dairy Queen and order the works. I mean everything—deluxe cheeseburger basket and shake, and even a hot-fudge sundae to top it off. But just as I'm starting in on my dessert, I notice Marcus and Tracie Nickerson coming in with a couple of youth group kids.

As they move toward the counter to place their order, I duck my head and, leaving my uneaten sundae behind, I slip out a side door, then hop on my bike and ride away. That was close. I'm not even sure why I feel so paranoid about seeing them, but somehow I know it could really screw this whole thing up for me.

I continue shooting pictures until about three o'clock, when I finally run out of film and decide that I should head back home. I know it seems crazy as I pedal back across town, but in some ways this has been a really good day. One of the best ones I've had in weeks. And yet I am totally miserable too. How weird is that?

When I get home, I am still full of energy. Maybe it's because of all the food I've consumed, or maybe it's because I know that this is my last day to be alive. But anyway, I suddenly decide that if I'm going out, I should go out in style, so I decide to straighten the house. I rearrange some of the furniture, hang scarves over the lamps, and move some more candles from my mom's bedroom out to the living room.

I even make my bed and do my laundry, folding everything and putting it all neatly away. I stand in the middle of my room for a while, just staring at everything. I wonder what Mom will do with my stuff. I decide to stick a note on my CD case saying that these are to be given to Carlie, since we both like the same kind of music and I think some of them might even be hers anyway. Then I make a note saying that Jonathan can have my classic sixties posters if he wants them. He told me once that he thought they were pretty cool, but he might've just been saying that to get on my good side.

Maybe the rest of my stuff will be taken to Goodwill. I pick up my old stuffed bear and hold him close. His name is Harry and I've had him for as long as I can remember. His chocolate-brown fur is a little matted and worn and he's missing his left eye, but I think he's beautiful. And he's been with me through so many things (like broken hearts and childhood illnesses) that I decide he should be with me when I check out of here. So I take him back into the living room and set him in the rocker. "You wait here," I tell him. And I feel some comfort in knowing that when I go to my final sleep, Harry will be in my arms. Maybe I will ask in my suicide note that we be buried together.

I hope I can remember to write all this down when the time comes. I hate to think of leaving anything undone. Well, besides my life, that is.

nine

IT'S NEARLY FIVE O'CLOCK WHEN I DECIDE THAT THE PLACE NEEDS SOME fresh flowers. So I take some scissors and a coffee can outside and start cutting tulips and daffodils and whatever I can find growing around our house. My grandma told me how she planted all these flowers back when she and my grandpa used to live in this house. But then Grandpa died and it wasn't long after that my dad left us and we moved in with her. And then she took off on her crazy road trip. But at least she had the foresight to plant all these flowers. And maybe it's me, but I think this is the best they've ever looked. That is, until I cut nearly all of them.

I've gathered quite a large bouquet by the time Grace's little red car pulls up in front of my house. I wave and walk over to meet her. I'm guessing by her determined expression that she hasn't changed her mind after all.

"What are you doing?" she asks as she walks into my yard.

"I thought we might like some flowers."

She nods. "That's a nice touch."

Then we go inside and I arrange the flowers in the biggest vase I can find and place them on the coffee table with the rest of my shrine, which I think is looking rather nice.

"That's pretty," says Grace as she sits on the couch. Then she opens her bag. "I brought some Jason mementos of my own too. I thought it'd be kind of cool to have them here."

"Good idea." I pick up my bear and sit in the rocking chair, watching as she carefully arranges what appear to be old concert-ticket stubs and a dried-up corsage that I'm guessing was from the winter dance, since she and Jason went together. She puts out several other things and then finally leans back and sighs. She looks somewhat uncomfortable as she glances around the room, crossing and uncrossing her long legs. Then she starts biting on her thumbnail.

"Are you nervous?" I finally ask.

"Yeah."

I look up at the clock to see that it's a little past five. "I wonder where Seth is."

"Do you think he's backing out?"

"I don't—"

Just then, there's a knock on the door, which actually makes me jump. "I don't know why I'm so uptight," I say as I get up to answer it. "It's like I think the cops are going to come in here and bust us or something."

This makes Grace laugh, just barely.

I crack the door to make sure that it's Seth before I open it wide and let him in. "We thought maybe you were chickening out on us," I say as he comes inside.

"No way," he says in a serious voice. "I just had to make a couple of stops on my way over here." Then he pulls a suspicious-looking Ziploc baggie from his inside pocket.

"Weed?" I say incredulously.

"Well, it's not oregano."

"You brought pot?" says Grace as she stands up and comes over to see for herself.

He holds up his bag like it's some kind of a trophy. "Only the very best too. I thought we might as well go out happy."

Grace is frowning.

"No," I tell Seth in my firmest voice. "We are *not* going to smoke pot and then kill ourselves. It will just make us all look stupid. People might even think that we were too high to know what we were doing."

Grace nods. "Yeah, that'd ruin everything, Seth. I don't want my parents thinking I had to do drugs to get up the nerve to do this."

"That's right," I agree. "Get rid of the weed, Seth."

Now he frowns as he slips it back into his pocket. "But this is two hundred bucks' worth of *good* stuff."

I just shake my head. "And don't leave it in your pocket either." Then I kind of laugh. "I mean, it's not like you're going to be needing it, you know. Not after tonight."

"That's right," says Grace. "And we don't want them finding that on you and getting all suspicious about us. Throw it away."

"Where?" he asks, looking around the room.

"Good point," I say. "We can't just put it in the trash. Someone might find it." I'm actually thinking that my brother Jonathan might come home and think he'd hit the jackpot.

"Do you have a garbage disposal?" asks Grace.

And soon we are all standing around the sink, watching as Seth dumps the weed down the churning disposal. By the time I turn off the switch, his expression is very sober.

"Man, there goes two hundred bucks down the drain," he says sadly.

"Hey, you can't take it with you," I tell him.

"Guess not."

We go back into the living room now and sit down. No one says anything and finally I can't stand the silence.

"Did you guys tell anyone where you are?" I suddenly ask them. I'm worried that someone might come looking for us and blow this whole thing.

"I told my mom I was spending the night with Lacy," says Grace. "And Lacy is going out with Ryan tonight. So I think I'm pretty safe."

"I told my parents that I was going to a friend's," says Seth. Then he looks down and shakes his head. "Like I have friends."

"We're your friends," I tell him.

He brightens. "Yeah, and Jason is too."

"And we'll all be together now," says Grace. But she is starting to cry again.

We talk some more about Jason and about what a sucky world we're living in and how Jason had it all figured out. We talk about how brave he was to go alone and we wonder if he will feel better when he finds out that we're joining him.

It bugs me that I don't really know where it is we'll be joining him. I mean, I used to believe in heaven, or at least I thought I did (although I've never been too sure about hell), but now it's like I don't believe in anything at all. All I can see is this big black hole waiting for us, and even though Seth keeps saying it will be great, I have to admit that I'm still a little unsure.

"Are you having second thoughts?" he asks me.

I shake my head. "Not really. I guess I just wonder where we'll be this time tomorrow."

"We'll be way better off than we are now," he assures me. "I know I can't stand to keep living like this."

"Me neither," says Grace as she wipes her nose.

"Yeah, me neither," I agree.

Then we decide to write our letters. We planned to write them all simultaneously at my house. This was to avoid the chance of either Seth's or Grace's family accidentally discovering our secret pact. So we all sit there quietly for about an hour, writing out our final words to our family and friends.

In my letter, I tell everyone that I love them. Including my brother, Jonathan. I also tell Jonathan that I'm sorry I told him that I hated him and that he was a loser and some other stupid things a couple of weeks ago. But I also tell him that I hope he'll get clean and stay clean. And I'm thinking this whole thing might actually help him. My death might even remind him that he's been throwing his own life away for the last couple of years.

Of course, this seems somewhat ironic, coming from someone who's about to commit suicide, but I don't allow myself to dwell on this too much. Then I mention the film from today's shooting spree. I tell my mom that I left it on my dresser, even explaining about my book idea and telling her that I hope she gets rich from it.

Finally we are all done. We put our letters into envelopes and set them on the coffee table.

"Want to order pizza?" asks Seth.

We all agree this is a good plan, and Seth even offers to buy. "I took a bunch of money out of my savings today," he tells us as he opens his wallet to a fat pile of twenties. "I would've gotten more, but the ATM has a limit."

"Why'd you do that?" asks Grace.

"I just thought I should have some fun on my last day," he tells us. "I went around town thinking I was going to buy whatever I wanted."

"What did you buy?" I ask.

"Nothing." He just shakes his head. "I guess I didn't really want anything after all."

Then we call up Domino's and order three different kinds of pizza. Everyone picks out their favorite. While we wait for the pizzas to be delivered, I put on some music and we light the candles again.

"My mom talked to Jason's mom today," says Seth.

"How's she doing?" I ask.

"Not too good. I guess she's mad at her husband, like maybe she thinks it's his fault that Jason did it or something."

"Why's that?" I ask.

"I don't know," he says. "My mom said that part of grieving is that you want to blame someone else for what happened."

I consider this and wonder who my mom will blame. Hopefully not Jonathan. If anyone, she should blame stupid Bradley. Not that it's really his fault. But he sure hasn't helped anything. Maybe she'll blame herself. Or me. Or maybe she'll blame my dad. Of course, he'll probably blame her right back. My head actually begins to hurt, and thankfully the pizza arrives and we are distracted by food. Our last supper.

I'm slightly disappointed that I don't have the same appetite I had earlier today. I'm full after just two slices. Grace and Seth don't seem to be very hungry either. Finally I wrap the leftovers in foil and put them in the fridge. I'm not even sure why I do this, but it just seems wasteful to throw it all away.

It's after seven and the sky is just getting dusky outside. Seth asks me to put on a CD that he brought over. There's a song he wants us to listen to. I think it's from the seventies, recorded by these two strange-looking guys named Simon and Garfunkel. The song is called "Sounds of Silence," and after listening to it several times, the words, "Hello darkness my old friend," become embedded in my brain. This inspires me to go around the house and close all the shades so that it's darker and to be sure that no one can look inside. I also check the locks on the doors and even secure the dead-bolts. We don't want any unexpected interruptions tonight.

Then I go back into the living room, where we all sit around the coffee table again. Seth takes out an extra large bottle of Tylenol and sets it on the table. And then Grace takes out a bottle that's the same size as mine and does the same. I reach into my pocket and remove my bottle and set it down too. Our weapons of choice, ready and loaded.

Then Seth clears his throat and says he'd like to read something. He takes out a couple pieces of notebook paper and proceeds to read what is a really beautiful poem. It's about friendship and loyalty and going the distance with each other.

Both Grace and I are crying by the time he finishes it.

"Did you write that?" asks Grace. But I know that he did because I know that Seth is a really good writer when he puts his mind to it. Jason was the first one to see this in him.

Seth nods as he refolds the sheets of notebook paper and replaces them in his pocket.

"Jason always thought you were a great writer," I say.

"Yeah, he's one of the few people who actually believed in me," says Seth.

"Hey, I believe in you," says Grace.

"Me too," I agree. And for the first time I realize what a cool guy Seth is and I wonder why I haven't been closer to him before. I guess the truth is that I used to judge him. I used to just assume that he was a loser and a freak without ever taking the time to really get to know him. Now I can see that he's really sensitive and deep.

"Should I put on some more music?" I ask.

"Yeah," says Grace, digging in her bag for something. "I brought a couple of CDs too."

So I go over and put four different CDs in the CD player. When I turn around, Seth is holding up his bottle of Tylenol, looking at it like he's ready.

"Do you think it's time?" asks Grace in a quiet voice.

Seth nods. "Yeah, I think so."

"We'll need some water," says Grace as she picks up her bottle of Tylenol.

So I go into the kitchen and fill three tall tumblers with water and take them back to the living room. "We might need more than this," I say suddenly. Then I go back to the kitchen and hunt until I find a large pitcher, and I fill it with more water and am just about to return to the living room when I hear the sound of a loud motor outside.

With shaking hands, I set down the pitcher and peek between the slats of the miniblinds in time to see a set of headlights pulling straight into our driveway, which runs alongside the house. It takes me a moment to figure out what this gigantic vehicle is, but suddenly I realize it's my grandma's Winnebago. I remember her message on the answering machine. How could I have missed that she meant she was coming *today*?

With a pounding heart I race back into the living room. "We have a problem," I tell them.

"What's wrong?" asks Seth.

"Company," I say quickly.

"Who's here?" asks Grace, her eyes wide with fear.

"My grandma."

Seth stands up and looks around desperately. "Can't you get rid of her, Morgan?"

I shake my head. "I seriously doubt it. She's in her motor home, which probably means she plans to stay for a few days."

"But why *now*?" demands Grace.

"I don't know," I tell her. "I only know that we can't do this tonight. Not with Grandma here. No way."

Seth grabs his Tylenol bottle and suicide letter. "I'm outta here."

"Me too," says Grace, following his lead.

"We'll call you, Morgan," says Seth as he heads for the door. "Don't worry. Maybe we can meet someplace later tonight to finish this."

"Okay," I say as they both shoot out to their cars.

But now I hear a loud knocking on the back door, and I know it's my grandma, and I know she probably has a key, and I am feeling totally spastic over her coming in here and seeing all this. How am I going to explain what we were doing? And how can I get rid of her so that we can finish? Most of all, how on earth can she possibly have such lousy timing?

ten

"GRANDMA!" I SAY, ACTING SURPRISED AS I OPEN THE DOOR. BUT INSTEAD of letting her inside, I step out to the back porch and close the door behind me. "What are you doing here?"

"Hi, Morgan," she says in her deep smoker's voice. "What's going on here?"

"Mom's gone," I say as if that should explain everything. Then I take her arm and start walking back toward her Winnebago.

"Where are you go—"

"I thought maybe we could talk in there," I say. "I mean, no one's home but me and I—"

"Who's inside the house?" she asks suspiciously.

"No one."

"Morgan," she says impatiently, "I know you've got someone in there. I saw two cars parked right out front."

"They're just leaving," I say as I wait in front of the door of her motor home.

"You having a party or something?" she asks as she opens the door and waits for me to go inside.

"Not exactly," I tell her.

"You better be straight with me, Morgan," she says in her no-nonsense voice.

"Can we sit down?" I ask.

She nods but still studies me with narrow-eyed suspicion as we sit down across from each other at her small Formica-topped dining table. I glance nervously around the interior of her motor home and feel surprisingly satisfied that very little has changed in here. The wooden cabinets all gleam as if she's just cleaned them, and I spy the built-in microwave, popcorn popper, coffee maker, and TV/VCR all secure in their proper places, all nice and neat. And then there's the musky smell of stale cigarette smoke. I kind of like it.

"I like it in here," I tell her. At least that's not a lie. Because despite my opinion about Grandma's crazy escapades, I've always loved her cozy Winnebago, and I used to think it would be fun to live in something small and compact like this someday.

Grandma nods in the direction of the house. "So, tell me the truth, Morgan. What exactly is going on in there? What is it that you're trying to keep from your old grandma?"

I take a deep breath. "It wasn't a party," I tell her. "But I did have a couple of friends over and . . ." I don't know what to say now, where to go from here.

"Were you kids drinking?" she asks as her penciled-in eyebrows draw together with concern.

I look down at the blue tabletop and just shake my head.

"Good grief, Morgan, please tell me you weren't doing drugs or anything stupid like that."

I look up to see that she's seriously worried now. "No, no, nothing like that," I assure her. "It's just that my friend Jason Harding died and—"

"The Harding boy?" she looks alarmed. "Oh, dear. What on earth happened to him?"

Without giving too much detail, I explain the suicide, and

Grandma looks truly grieved. "Oh, dear. That's just terribly sad," she says as she shakes her head. "What an awful shame."

"And we were just having kind of a memorial thing for him," I tell her. "And we had candles lit and stuff and I guess I thought it might seem weird, you know. And it startled me when you knocked on the door."

She nods, but I'm not sure that she's entirely convinced.

"I'm just so sad about the whole thing, Grandma," I tell her. "I miss him so much." And suddenly I am crying all over again.

She reaches across the table and takes both my hands in hers and just squeezes them gently. "Death is hard, Morgan. And it hurts even worse when someone takes his own life. Oh, I'm so sorry for you, dear."

We talk for a while longer and then I realize that I need to invite her back into the house. I just hope I can get into the living room and pick up my suicide letter and Tylenol bottle before she sees them.

"Do you want to come inside?" I finally ask.

"Sure," she says. "I like my little Winnebago just fine, but I thought it'd be nice to be in a real house for a while."

So I lead the way, and while she's getting herself a drink of water in the kitchen I manage to hurry into the living room to remove the questionable items. So other than the burning candles and our somewhat strange looking shrine to Jason, everything looks fairly normal.

Grandma comes in and looks at the photos of Jason that are still spread across the table, then she picks up yesterday's newspaper and skims the article about Jason, shaking her head again.

"Such a shame and a waste," she says as she sinks down into the couch. "Young people have so much ahead of them. I just don't understand why anyone with so much to look forward to would take his own life."

I nod as if I agree with her. And on some levels I suppose I do. I mean, I don't really understand it either. And yet . . .

"I don't know too much about these things," she continues in a sad voice, "but it seems to me that if God is the one who gives us our lives, then he should be the one who decides when it's time to take them back again."

I am somewhat surprised by this. "Since when did you start believing in God?" I ask her.

She sort of laughs. "Oh, I've got lots to tell you, Morgan. Lots and lots."

You and me both. Not that I plan to tell her anything about the suicide pact. But other things. And so I begin by telling her what her only daughter is doing right now.

"Oh, dear," she says after I finish my story. "Lee Anne mentioned a new boyfriend last month, but I had no idea that it had gone this far."

"And he's barely older than me and Jonathan," I tell her. "He's like twenty-something."

She makes a tsk-tsk sound and shakes her head again. "When are the newlyweds supposed to be back anyway?"

"Tomorrow," I say, suddenly remembering how I had planned for them to find us.

"Where's Jonathan?" she asks.

"Who knows?"

She presses her lips together as if she's disappointed. "Is he still messing with those despicable drugs?"

I roll my eyes as I nod.

"Too bad. And I've really been praying for him too."

"You pray now?"

"Oh, yes. I've discovered it's the only way to go." Then she smiles at me. "And I have you to thank for some of this, Morgan. Remember that Christmas card you sent me?"

I sigh. "Yeah, sort of." Last December, I got all freaked out about my grandma. I'd heard about another motor home that had slid off a mountain road during an ice storm and everyone inside had been killed. As a result I wrote Grandma this crazy letter, begging her to accept Jesus as her personal Savior before it was too late. Like I thought she was going to kick the bucket or something. The whole thing seems pretty lame to me now, especially as I finger the Tylenol bottle in my pocket and consider what I had been planning on doing tonight.

"Well, I was staying in this RV park just outside of Las Vegas during Christmastime," she continues. "My regular motor home friends were all there and we'd all gone to a casino together," she chuckles. "And that was on Christmas Eve too. Oh, we'd been drinking and gambling and carousing, and as I went inside my motor home, something just hit me. All at once it seemed that everything was so empty and shallow and I began to wonder if that was all there was to life. And I sat up late into the night, just looking out the window toward the desert and up at the stars and I kept asking myself if this was all there was. And if this was all there was, well, I wondered, what was the point?"

"*Really?*" Despite myself, not to mention my thwarted plan to end my own life, I feel somewhat curious about Grandma's experience that night.

She nods. "Yes. So the next day—it was Christmas Day—well, I packed up and started my engine and just began driving. I wasn't even sure where I was going, but I was determined to go somewhere.

Finally I came to this little old church out in the country all by itself, and I saw some other cars and pickups parked around it, so I decided to park my Winnebago in front and go in."

I try to imagine this. My smoking, drinking, gambling, rough-talking grandma pulling her big motor home up in front of a little country church and then just walking in. I wonder if she'd been wearing one of her bright-colored jogging suits like the purple and pink one that she's wearing right now.

"Well, they were already into their church service, but I found a seat in the back and started to listen. And I'll tell you what, Morgan, it was as if the good Lord himself was talking to me. I just sat there, taking in every word with my mouth hanging open."

"Seriously?"

She nods and continues. "And then the pastor invited people to come forward and pray with him. And I just got right up from that pew and walked to the front." She chuckles now. "Just me and a gawky young red-headed girl went up. But the pastor led us in a prayer and we invited Jesus into our hearts. Just like that, your old grandma got herself saved."

I sigh and try to look happy for her. But deep down I feel sick. Sick and tired.

"That's all I get from you?" she asks. "I thought you'd be jumping up and down with joy, Morgan. I came all this way just to tell you the news myself."

"That's nice, Grandma."

"That's nice, Grandma?" she repeats in a loud raspy voice, looking at me as if I might have two heads. "What on earth is wrong with you, girl? I thought you'd be—" Then she stops herself. "Oh, dear. I'm so sorry, Morgan. I temporarily forgot about your friend. How selfish of me."

"That's okay." Now I just want to end this conversation. Just do what it takes to get her to stop talking and go back out to her motor home.

"Yes, I can certainly understand how it's hard to get excited about anything right now. You poor thing. You've been through a lot. And staying here all by yourself. Well, no wonder you needed to have a few friends over." Then she frowns. "And then here I come breaking up the party."

"It wasn't a party."

"I know, I know." She waves her hand. "How about if I go back out to my Winnebago and you call your friends and finish up whatever it was you were doing?" She's standing now, like she's ready to go.

"No, that's okay," I tell her, not wanting to seem too impolite. "I think we might've been done for the night anyway."

She looks at her watch. "But it's not even nine o'clock yet. I know that must be early for you young people."

"Really," I tell her, glancing nervously at the phone now. "It's okay. We were done." Even so, I wish she would leave. But she just sits back down and continues her story where she left off. Her cheerful chatter grates on my nerves now, and it feels like her words are bouncing off the walls in the living room.

"Well, I have to admit that I wasn't completely sure that it was the real thing at first," she says, comfortably settling herself into the sofa. "I guess I'm just an old skeptic at heart. I got to thinking that maybe I was just having an emotional experience that would fade away in time. So I asked the pastor if it would be okay for me to park my motor home at the church, just until the next service, you know. He's such a nice man, he said it would be perfectly fine. Why, he even let me hook up to their electricity and water—although I paid them later."

For some reason this captures my attention. "You mean you *camped* at the church?"

She grins and nods. "I went to the next Sunday service and then to the Wednesday service and then I did the same thing all over again the next week. And those sweet church people sort of adopted me, just took me right into their hearts. I was invited into their homes and I kept going to church. Every single time the doors were open, I was there. And before I knew it I had been there for more than two whole months. Can you believe it? Your grandma turned into a church lady."

"So you gave up your smoking and drinking and gambling?" I ask.

"No more drinking and gambling for Grandma." She smiles somewhat sheepishly. "But the smoking's still a challenge. Although, Pastor Larson assures me that God loves me whether or not I smoke. That's a huge relief. And, as the Good Book says, Rome wasn't built in a day."

"That's in the Bible?"

"Well, maybe not. I've still got a lot to learn, Morgan."

"But what made you decide to come here all of a sudden?" I ask, curious about her ironic sense of timing.

"Like I said, I wanted to tell you the good news. But besides that, I just felt like I needed to come. I think maybe it was the Lord's leading. Darned, I wish I'd come a day or two sooner. Then I could've been here before your friend died and before your mom and her young man ran off and eloped like a couple of harebrained idiots."

"Well, you're here now," I say. And it seems she has no intention of leaving either. But I notice that I'm beginning to relax a little. Like maybe it's not such a bad thing she showed up.

"Yes, I guess that's what counts. But I still feel bad to have interrupted you and your friends like—"

"Don't worry about it, Grandma," I say quickly.

We talk some more and when Grandma mentions she's hungry,
I offer her some of our leftover last-supper pizza. She eats several
pieces and I eat part of one, just to be polite, and then she
announces that she's going to bed.

"I suppose you could sleep in the house," I offer without enthusiasm. "I mean, Jonathan's room is a disaster area, but maybe you
could sleep in Mom's—"

"No, no," she says. "I'm more comfortable in my own bed."

"Okay."

And then we say goodnight. At first I'm relieved that she's gone,
but after she returns to her RV, I begin to feel very much alone
again. I pace for a while, then decide to call Grace and Seth to see
if they went home. I feel bad that Grandma's unexpected appearance ruined everything. But neither of them are home and I don't
have Grace's cell phone number. It worries me that they haven't
gone home. I wonder what they're doing right now. What if they're
going to carry out the suicide pact without me? Or what if they've
already done it?

eleven

I TRY TO PUSH THOUGHTS OF GRACE AND SETH FROM MY MIND AS I BLOW out the candles. Then I move all the Jason memorabilia into my room, reverently rearranging these precious items on my dresser. I want to put our house back to its normal order. No reason to give my mom something to question me about when she and Bradley get home tomorrow. If I'm still here, that is.

I turn off most of the lights and begin to pace some more. It's nearly eleven now and I haven't heard a word from Grace or Seth. I have the worst feeling that they may have continued this whole thing without me. Maybe they went to a park or rented a hotel room. After all, Seth had a wallet full of cash. I feel more left behind than ever now. Not only is Jason gone, but it's possible that Seth and Grace are on their way out too. As bizarre as it seems, I feel betrayed by this possibility, even though I felt just a tiny bit relieved when my grandma showed up. I feel more frustrated than ever, like my escape plan has been totally messed up. And it's so scary to think that I may have to just go on like this—living in such hopeless darkness and feeling this pain that never seems to go away.

I go into my room, where I light one dark red candle and set it on my dresser. Then I sit down on my bed and take the slightly crumpled suicide note from my pocket. I try to flatten it with my hands before I set it alongside the Jason shrine on top of my dresser.

Then I take the Tylenol bottle out of my pocket and open it. It's still nearly full of those precious white caplets. And they seem to be promising me that my troubles can end right here and now if I want them to. It's like they're whispering to me, gently telling me that I will finally be able to go to sleep. That I'll finally find rest and peace and just forget about everything. Oh, it sounds so good. So tempting.

I pour some of these lovely white pills into the palm of my hand and just look at them, studying the small pile until it grows blurry and I realize that my eyes are full of tears again. Something in me is not ready. I find this very hard to believe. It's like I've got this huge boulder pinning me down to the ground and when someone offers to remove it, I'm telling them, "No, wait. I'm not ready to feel relief yet." It makes no sense.

Even so, I put the caplets back into the bottle, replace the child-proof cap, and set it on the dresser right next to the letter. Then I stand there just staring at it. Why am I unable to do this? What am I waiting for? Why not just give up? Just get it over with?

Suddenly I am down on my knees and I am crying and sobbing. And then it's like I'm exploding, ranting and raging like a wild animal. I pound my fists into my bed and my pillows, harder and harder, as if I want to kill someone. Maybe just me. I carry on like this for quite a while until I am exhausted and slightly worried that my grandma might hear me.

Calmer now, I get up and begin to pace again. My heart is still pounding, but my mind is slightly clearer. And now it's racing, wondering what's happening with Grace and Seth, wondering if they may already be dead, or nearly dead. How long does it take to die from a Tylenol overdose anyway?

Just then the phone rings and I race through the darkened

house and without even checking the caller ID, I pick it up.

"Morgan, this is Seth."

"Seth!" I say with relief. "Where are you? What's up?"

"We're down at the park," he says. "We were just talking and trying to figure out what to do. Is your grandma still there?"

"Yeah. She's going to be here for a while."

"That's what we thought."

"You guys aren't going to do it right now, are you?" I ask. "I mean, not without me."

"No way," he assures me. "You're part of this, Morgan. You loved Jason just as much as we did and—" He pauses. "Grace wants to talk to you."

"Hey," says Grace in a soft voice. "How's it going?"

"Okay, I guess. I'm just relieved that you guys didn't, you know, do it without me."

"Don't worry," she says. "We won't. But I just got an idea. I haven't even told Seth about it yet. What do you guys think about waiting until the day of Jason's funeral? I mean, that way we could go to it, and we'd have more time to plan this whole thing better, so that it doesn't get messed up, you know?"

"I like that," I say. "I mean, I hadn't really considered it before, but it might be important to go to the funeral. What does Seth think?"

"Here," she says. "I'll let him talk to you."

"I'm not so sure," he says. "I keep getting this feeling that we should be with Jason right now, you know. Like maybe he needs us or something."

I consider this. "Yeah, I kind of know what you mean. But I like Grace's idea too. Don't you think that Jason would appreciate it if we hung around long enough to go to his funeral?"

There's a long pause now. Then finally Seth talks. "Yeah, you might be right. And since you both seem to agree . . . yeah, well, maybe we should just wait."

"Okay." And yet even as I agree, I am feeling like Jason's funeral is a long way out there. I seriously wonder if I can hang on that long.

"Grace says to take care," Seth tells me.

"Yeah, you guys too." I sigh. "Sorry that things went kind of sideways tonight."

"Yeah, me too. I was looking forward to moving on, ya know."

"Me too."

"But maybe it's better this way."

"Yeah," I say halfheartedly. "Maybe."

We hang up and I feel this mixture of confusion and disappointment. In a way I guess I'm slightly relieved that the pressure is off, at least for tonight. And at least I know that Seth and Grace haven't done it without me. But at the same time I'm not sure how I can live with this aching pain that keeps twisting and turning inside of me. I understand what Seth meant about moving on. I mean, I really thought everything would all be over and done with by now. I thought that by now I'd be asleep, blissfully asleep, with Harry in my arms and my two friends by my side and that soon we would be with Jason.

Instead, I am all alone in my house and I'm afraid that I will never be able to fall asleep again. I consider doing the vodka trick for a second time, but somehow knowing that my grandma's right next door and that my mom will be home tomorrow . . . well, I'm not sure. I'm just not sure about anything.

With the lights still out, I pace and pace all around my darkened house until I feel like maybe I am actually going crazy, and I seriously wonder if someone should come take me away, like maybe I should be locked up in a padded cell somewhere. I mean, it's like I can't even think straight anymore. Sometimes I think I'm talking to Jason and then I think I'm talking to God, and then I realize that I'm just ranting to myself like a mad woman.

I walk in and out of the rooms of my silent house and desperately try to figure things out, try to make sense of what's going on inside me. I consider calling someone for help, but who would I call at this hour? And what would I tell them? And what good would it do anyway? I am so confused. So lost. It's like my brain has been totally tumbled and spun and hung out to dry. And I am so tired. So very, very tired. Yet I know I can't sleep.

Finally, I am so pathetically desperate that I wander outside and find myself just standing out there in my bare feet in our graveled driveway. First I look up at the sky, as if there is something or someone up there who might be able to help me. And then I look at the motor home, wondering if my grandma has gone to bed yet.

I'm not sure how long I stand out there, shivering in the coolness of the spring night, but finally I notice that it looks like a light is on inside the Winnebago, and so I knock quietly on the door.

"Morgan, is that you?" The door opens just a crack.

"Sorry to bother you," I say, suddenly feeling foolish for acting like such a neurotic baby. But I can't help it.

"Come inside," she says, quickly opening the door wider. She's wearing a pink fuzzy bathrobe and has green sponge curlers in her hair and some kind of cream on her face. If I didn't know she was my own grandma, I might actually be frightened by her appearance.

"I really need to talk to someone," I tell her.

"Have a seat," she says, pointing to the couch as she sits down in the easy chair across from it.

I sit on the couch, pulling her bright orange-and-green striped afghan around my shoulders, and I try to figure out where to begin. Or maybe I should just leave and keep my mouth shut.

"What's up?" she asks, studying me carefully. "Are you feeling bad about Jason?"

I nod without speaking. There's a lump about the size of an apple in my throat.

Then she comes over and sits on the couch beside me. She puts her arm around me and gently squeezes me into her soft robe. "I know it's hard, Morgan," she says in a calming voice. "But God can help you through it."

Yeah, sure, like God helped Jason?

"And I know it seems hard to believe, but it will get better in time, dear."

"What if it doesn't?" I manage to mutter. "I mean, I know some kids who are so bummed about Jason that they're thinking about following his example and doing the same—"

"You can't be serious, Morgan." Grandma sits up straight and stares at me with a horrified expression.

I blink as I realize what I've just said. How stupid could I be?

"Morgan," she peers at me closely. "Do you mean that you actually know kids who are considering suicide too?"

I look down at my lap now, watching as my fingers weave in and out of the loopy holes of the afghan. Oh, why did I come out here tonight? What is wrong with me?

"Morgan, you can tell me," she says in a persuasive tone. "Do you really know someone who's seriously considering suicide?"

Maybe I'm weak, or pathetic, or on the verge of losing my mind, but without looking up I just nod. I silently give in.

"But surely they don't really want to do something like that, do they? Of course these kids must feel very sad about losing a dear friend, but surely they must realize that suicide is not the answer. Don't they?"

Now I'm crying again. "I—I don't know. I mean, it probably doesn't make sense to you. But everything seems so hopeless . . . and I kind of understand how they feel."

"Of course, you do, dear. But I'm sure you'd never consider anything like that yourself."

I just shrug now. Okay, maybe I'm embarrassed to admit that not only have I considered it, but I'd have gone through with it tonight had she not come and screwed it all up. "I'm not so sure, Grandma. I guess I'm not sure about much of anything anymore."

"But what about your faith in God?" she asks. "How do you think God would feel about it?"

"I haven't really been talking to God much lately."

She makes her tsk-tsk sound now. "Well, that explains a lot. How can you, or anyone else for that matter, expect to make it through something as hard as this without talking to God? Why, I've only been a Christian for two and a half months, and even I know that much."

"I'm a mess," I admit as I wipe my nose on my sweatshirt sleeve. "Everything seems so hopeless. It's like I'm in this black hole and I can't find my way out."

"You know what they say: It's always darkest before the dawn."

"Well, it just keeps getting darker and darker for me," I tell her. "And I have friends—" I choke on this—"friends who are ready to give up." The thought of Seth and Grace makes me sob even harder. I'm worried that they might change their minds and do this thing tonight after all—maybe down there in the park, or maybe they'll find some really secluded place where their bodies wouldn't be found for days. And then I'd be left behind to suffer alone. I just can't take it.

Grandma sits up straighter now, and turning me toward her she looks directly into my face. "Are you talking about a *suicide pact*?" she asks with worried eyes. "I saw a show on Oprah once where they talked about this very thing."

I kind of shrug, then say, "I guess it might be something like that." Still, I don't admit my own involvement. How can I? Even so, I do let it slip that those are the same friends who were at my house last night, the ones who took off when she arrived.

"I scared them off?"

"Sort of."

"Do you honestly think these friends of yours would really go through with something like that?"

"I—I don't know," I gulp. "I mean . . . I think they would. But I think they'd wait until after Jason's funeral."

"Are you absolutely sure about this?" She stands, then hands me a Kleenex. "Because a suicide threat is the kind of thing you should take seriously."

I nod as I blow my nose. "I am taking it seriously."

Grabbing several Kleenexes, she begins wiping the cream from her face. "And if you're this concerned for your friends, well, my goodness, don't you think we should do something? Something to stop them?"

Now I am really worried. I'm afraid I've said way too much. "Oh, I don't know."

She gasps. "Well, think about it, Morgan. If your friends are really serious about this—this suicide pact—don't you think we should take action? I think we should call the police right now."

"But what if they're not really serious?" I say quickly. "What if we call the police and just get them into trouble?" Now I am feeling totally freaked out. I mean, no way am I going to rat on my friends, especially knowing that if they go down, I'll go down with them. Somehow I have to stop whatever it is I've put into motion here.

"I shouldn't have said anything," I say quickly. "I think I'm just tired and emotional right now."

"It was right that you told me," she insists. "What if they're doing something dangerous right now? Wouldn't it be better for them to get into a little bit of trouble and then get some help?"

I take a deep breath. "I really don't think we need to worry about this tonight." I am using the calmest voice I can manage. "I appreciate your concern, Grandma, but I think I just needed someone to talk to and I'm sure I've overblown the whole thing."

"But you're the one who came in here," she says. "All worked up over this—"

"I know," I say, hoping she'll buy it. "And I'm really, really sorry. I just felt kind of confused and upset and I guess I just needed to talk to someone."

She plops down on the couch beside me and takes my hand in hers. "Okay, Morgan, if you think your friends are going to be alright for now."

"I think they're alright, Grandma. As alright as they can be, I mean. I think we're all feeling pretty upset right now." I actually force a small pathetic smile to my lips.

"Okay, then." She looks up at the clock. "Oh, my! It's one o'clock in the morning. I had no idea it was so late!"

"I'm sorry I disturbed—"

"Nonsense," she says. "I think we should both go to bed. And I think that you should sleep in the RV with me. No sense in you being all by yourself in that old house."

And so it is that I am tucked into bed, right next to my grandma, and it's not long before the madness of the world begins to fade away and I actually fall asleep. But even as I'm drifting I find myself wishing that it was a complete sleep—one that I would never have to awaken from.

***

But I do wake up, and it's to the sound of someone talking. I open my eyes to see that it's daylight now, and I can hear my grandma's voice and it sounds like she's talking to someone on the phone.

"Yes, Morgan is here," she is saying. "Let me see if she's awake."

"I'm awake," I moan as I reach for the phone.

She's holding her hand over the phone as if she doesn't want the person on the other end to hear. "It's the police, dear."

I sit up straight in bed. *The police?*

She nods. "I got up early this morning and felt concerned for your friends and their suicide pact. I just thought we should let someone in authority know."

I close my eyes and wish I were dead.

"I hope you don't mind," she says with a slightly apologetic smile.

twelve

"IS THIS MORGAN BERGSTROM?" ASKS A STRANGE VOICE.

"Yes," I mumble.

"I need you to give me the names of your friends," he says. "The kids involved in the suicide pact."

"But I can't do that," I say.

"I know you probably think you're doing them a favor," he continues. "But believe me, the best thing you can do is turn them in so they can get the help they need."

I fall back down into the pillows on my grandma's bed and groan.

"Is this a bad time?" he asks.

"Yes!" I snap. "It's a very bad time."

"I'm sorry."

The gentleness in his voice makes me feel guilty. "Look," I tell him. "I'm not even out of bed yet. I can't think right now."

"Okay," he says. "I understand. Why don't you get up and I'll be in contact with you later today."

"Yeah, sure," I say. *"Fine."*

"We really need your cooperation if we're going to help these kids," he says. I hang up and groan again.

"Something wrong?" asks Grandma as I give the phone back to her.

I pull the pillow over my head and make a growling noise that sounds like some wild animal. Then I sit up and look at her. "This is just turning into such a mess," I say.

"Some things have to get messy before they can be cleaned up."

"I can't rat on my friends, Grandma. They'll get mad at me."

"Not once they realize that you're just trying to help them."

"Who's going to help *me*?" I say as I get out of bed.

She smiles. "Well, I will. And then, of course, there's God."

"Yeah, right."

But Grandma ignores my skepticism. Instead she tells me to go into the house and take a shower and get dressed. "And I will fix us both some breakfast."

"What about the police?" I ask.

"Don't worry about that for now," she says. "Let's just take this one step at a time. Right now, you need to take a shower and wake up."

So, relieved to be told what to do, I follow her instructions, and when I finish up and come into the kitchen, she is handing a strange man a cup of coffee.

"This is Detective Mason," Grandma says as I sit down at the table. "And this is Morgan."

I push a wet strand of hair away from my face and look at the gray-haired man. I wonder if he is going to arrest me for not cooperating with him. I'm not even sure if I care.

"Sorry to interrupt your breakfast like this," he says as Grandma sets a plate of eggs and toast in front of me.

"Whatever." I don't feel a bit hungry, but I pick up a piece of toast and take a tiny nibble.

He makes small talk as I try to look like I'm eating, but I finally just take my plate over to the sink and dump it. Then I slowly pour myself a cup of coffee and carefully add milk, all the while considering making a break for the back door and running far, far away from here. But, really, what's the use? Where would I go? What difference would it make? I finally return to my chair at the table and, feeling like a prisoner, sit down and wait.

"Ready to talk?" asks the detective.

"What is it you want from me?" I try not to look directly at him as I take a sip of coffee. I want to appear cool and calm, like this is no big deal, but the truth is, I want to scream.

He opens a little black notebook and then asks if I know for a fact that there really is a suicide pact.

I shrug and stare down at the table.

"Holding back information won't help anyone."

I close my eyes and wish that he would just go away and leave me alone. But when I open my eyes, he's still there, just patiently sitting at our kitchen table and studying me. "I know this isn't easy," he says. "But I think you'll be glad that you helped your friends. A suicide pact can really spin out of control. It can get very ugly."

"Did you see it on Oprah too?" I ask, knowing that I must sound belligerent.

He looks slightly confused, but then Grandma explains.

"Morgan," she says to me. "You need to cooperate with Detective Mason. Just give him the names of the kids who are in danger. All he wants to do is help them."

"That's right," he says.

"It's not like they have anything written in stone," I say. "It's just that some—uh—some friends of mine were pretty bummed about Jason, you know. And I guess that suicide just seemed like a nice escape plan."

"Do you know exactly how many kids are involved?"

"Just two or three." Now I look away, certain that this cop can see right through me. I mean, what am I doing here? Sitting in my own kitchen and lying to a detective? What is wrong with me? But how can I cooperate?

Then he asks me once more to tell him the names.

"I can't—can't do that," I stammer.

He sighs. "I understand that you think you may be protecting them, Morgan. But you need to know that we only want to help. We're not the enemy, you know."

I look at him. He probably means well, but I'm not convinced. Besides, how can I rat on Seth and Grace without incriminating myself too? And how hypocritical would it be to pretend that I'm not involved?

"Is there some kind of law?" I ask him. "That says I have to give you their names?"

He sort of smiles now. "Not exactly. But if something happens to your friends and you withhold information that could've prevented it . . . well, there might be people who would try to prosecute you."

I feel my eyes opening wide now. "Seriously?"

He nods. "Law is a funny thing, Morgan. It's usually interpreted in the courtroom. We law officers just try to enforce it the best we can. Mostly we want to protect people—people like your friends. If you care about them, you'll want to help them too."

"It's the right thing to do, Morgan," says my grandma. "Come on, dear, you won't be sorry. Not in the long run."

"She's right," says the detective.

Now I can feel my hands starting to shake. I try to conceal it by wrapping them both around my warm coffee cup, but I can see the surface of the liquid jiggling.

"Will you give me their names now?"

"Look," I tell him. "They're not planning to do it until after Jason's funeral. What if you give me a chance to talk to them first, to sort of warn them, you know—"

"The only problem with that is that it could trigger something," he explains. "It might push them to do it sooner. It would really be better if you just tell me their names. Then we can speak to their families and see about getting them some help, some counseling perhaps." He peers at me now and I suspect he's thinking the same thing about me.

"Are you going to lock them up?"

He smiles now, but it's a sad smile. "Not if we don't think they're in real danger."

"Do you think they're in danger?"

"What do *you* think?" He's peering closely at me now, like maybe he suspects I'm not telling him everything.

I look back at him evenly. "I think that living is dangerous."

"And what about *dying*?" he asks.

I don't answer.

Then he questions me about the method they planned to use to carry out their pact and I tell him about the Tylenol. He doesn't even seem the least bit surprised by this as he makes more notes in his black notebook.

"Morgan," says Grandma as she places her hand on my shoulder. "This is very serious, dear."

"I really need those names, Morgan." The detective sounds like he's getting tired of waiting.

So, feeling like a robot who's been programmed to speak, I finally say Grace's and Seth's names and I sit there watching as he writes them down. I suddenly feel like a loser and a hypocrite and I'd do anything to take back my words and just take off running from my house, never to be seen again.

"And no one else is involved?"

I swallow against the lump that's growing in my throat as I look down at my coffee cup, but I just shake my head in answer. How I long for a stone to crawl under.

"And these kids were at your house?" he continues. "Just last night?"

The kitchen is silent as I nod, but I still don't look at him or Grandma.

"I saw the two cars when I got here," Grandma confirms with enthusiasm. "I thought Morgan was having a party or something."

"Yeah," I say sarcastically. "We were having a really great time."

"And you know for a fact that both Seth and Grace are planning to commit suicide?" asks the detective. I can tell he is watching me closely now.

"I don't know anything for sure," I say in frustration. "Isn't it enough that I gave you their names? Can't you leave me alone now? I feel like I'm on trial here."

"But you're sure they wouldn't do it until after the funeral?" he continues, his steel blue eyes boring into me now. "Is that their plan, Morgan?"

"I don't know!" I say loudly. "I don't know anything anymore."

"Do you mean you don't know if they really plan to commit suicide or you don't know if they plan to wait until the day of the funeral?" he asks.

"I mean *I don't know anything*," I hear the irritation in my voice. I'm sure that everyone else hears it too. Why can't he just leave me alone? Why can't everyone just leave me alone?

"Okay, then let me ask you this. Do you plan to join your friends? Are you part of the pact?"

The silence in the kitchen is so thick that I feel like I can hardly breathe. I look up to Grandma and then back to the detective, then down at the coffee cup that has grown lukewarm in my hands.

"Morgan?" says Grandma. "You need to answer Detective Mason's question, dear."

"Do I plan on killing myself?" I say the words slowly as if I am trying to process their meaning. As if this is a completely new idea to me.

"Yes," he says. "That's what I need to know."

I shrug, wondering what the reaction will be if I answer this honestly. Will I be locked up? Finally, I decide to take the easy route to hopefully get these people off my case. "No, of course not," I tell them.

Grandma pats me on the back. "Of course, you wouldn't do that, dear."

"So you don't think suicide is a good idea?" he asks.

"Not so much." I try to make my face look hopeful, although I'm sure it looks pretty pathetic. "I mean, it might've seemed worth considering when they were here last night. But I have to admit it seems pretty whacked right now." The detective makes some more notes and I wonder if he really believes me.

"But what if your friends pressured you?" he asks. "What if they still plan to carry this through? Would you feel the need to join them?"

I don't answer. I just roll my eyes and wish he'd leave.

"Peer pressure can be overwhelming," he says, and I want to ask him if he's really a shrink in disguise, but I keep my mouth firmly shut. He just nods and makes some more notes. I can only imagine what he's writing about me. Then he asks me several more questions and finally seems satisfied. Or nearly. "But really,

Morgan," he says. "I'm concerned about you."

"About me?" I echo in a small voice.

"I'm still worried that you're at risk. Can you look me in the eyes and tell me that you're not planning to kill yourself?"

I simply shrug. "Not today."

"Then you haven't ruled it out completely?"

I sigh. "To be perfectly honest, I don't know how I feel about much of anything at the moment. I'm still really sad about Jason." I choke slightly now. "And I don't understand why he did it, and I just really miss him."

"Enough to follow his example?"

Grandma stands behind me now, putting both hands on my shoulders. "Morgan's been through a lot," she tells him. "But I'm sure she realizes that suicide is not the answer." She bends down and looks at me. "Don't you, Morgan?"

I nod as tears streak down my cheeks.

"Because we could have you placed in the Manchester Unit," he says. "They have a good psychiatrist and staff that know just how to—"

"I don't need to be locked up," I say quickly.

"And I'm here with her now," says Grandma. "She was all alone, you know, when this happened. It only makes sense that she would be very upset. If you want to put someone in the psychiatric unit, I suggest you go speak to those other two kids."

He nods. "Will you keep us informed?" he asks as he closes his notebook, then pulls out two business cards and hands one to Grandma. "If you think of anything, or hear anything, or learn of any other kids who might be considering something like this?" He slides the other card across the table and I stare at it without pick-ing it up. "Can you do that for me, Morgan?"

"Okay," I say, but even as I say it, I'm not so sure. Already I know that I've gotten Seth and Grace into trouble, and I know they're going to be furious. I also know that it's not going to go well for me either. I mean, I wouldn't be surprised if Detective Mason goes out to his car and orders someone from the Manchester Unit to come pick me up. Maybe it would be a relief. Maybe a straight jacket would be comforting. I feel more hopeless now than I did yesterday. But I try not to show it. I just want him to leave.

Detective Mason finally stands up. "Kids think it's an easy way out, but they don't realize that suicide really hurts a whole lot of people."

"And it doesn't solve a thing," says my grandma as she puts his empty cup in the sink.

"You folks take care now," he says as he heads out the back door.

After he leaves, Grandma looks at the clock and asks me which church I go to.

"Church?" I say the word as if I've never gone before.

"Yes, Morgan. Which church do you attend?"

I reluctantly tell her and she announces that we are going.

"But it's on the other side of town," I protest. "We don't even have a car."

"I have wheels," she says in a triumphant voice.

And so it is that I arrive at New Life Center in a Winnebago. Grandma parks her rig in the back of the parking lot and I walk beside her like someone going to the executioner. Attending church is about the last thing I want to do right now. But, like so many other things, it seems I have no choice. And I suppose it could be worse. I could be locked up in the Manchester Unit.

I'm barely inside when I notice Jason's family just making their way through the big double doors and, despite myself, I cannot help but stare at them. I mean, it's so weird, like they all look so nice and normal in their fashionable clothes and expensive shoes. It's like it's just another day at church for them. I almost wonder if this whole thing with Jason really happened or not. But then he's not there with them either. Jason's siblings, Jessica and Aaron, go down the aisle first. They must have come home from college because of Jason. They are followed by their parents. I can see Mrs. Harding's eyes as she removes her sunglasses and suddenly I know that this is not just another day in church. This woman is really suffering; pain is etched into her face. I look a little harder and I realize that they're all probably hurting. And I feel guilty for having judged them like that. What do I know anyway?

"Morgan," Mrs. Harding says when she sees me just inside the doorway. "How are you doing?"

I blink back tears. "Uh, not so great, I guess."

She nods. "None of us are."

"I have some photos," I say suddenly. "Recent ones that I took of Jason. Some of them are pretty good."

Her eyes light up a little.

"I thought you might like to have them."

"We would love to have copies," she says. "Come by the house anytime and bring them with you."

And then Mr. Harding takes her arm and begins ushering her down the aisle to their regular seats.

At the beginning of the service, Pastor Orlander mentions Jason's death and how the whole church family and community is grieving for him. Then he announces that Jason's memorial service will be Tuesday morning.

I sit there like a lump on the pew, considering that I might actually be better off locked up in the Manchester Unit right now, because I really feel like something may be seriously wrong with me. I feel like such an alien, like I don't belong here at all. Not in this church or this town or even on this planet. I avoid eye contact with Marcus and Tracie. I have no desire to speak to them or anyone. Finally I just start to imagine that I'm invisible and then blind, deaf, and dumb, and I let the words of the sermon just float right over me, like I'm not even here at all.

At some point, it occurs to me that this state of nonfeeling, this sense of nonexisting, is almost like being dead. Or perhaps I'm dying right now. What a relief that would be. Maybe it's not too late after all.

thirteen

AFTER WE GET HOME FROM CHURCH, I TELL MY GRANDMA THAT I WANT
to take a bike ride by myself. I tell her that I need to think and to
process some of the things I heard in church this morning. Yeah, right.

"Are you sure you want to go off all by yourself like that?" she
asks in a somewhat suspicious voice.

"It's okay, Grandma," I assure her. "Really, I'm not going to do
myself in. I promise."

She studies me, then finally nods. "Well, don't be gone too long,
honey. Or I'll start worrying."

It's cloudy and gray as I ride over to River Park. I vaguely wonder if it's going to rain, and then I wonder why I even care. I walk
my bike over to a spot near the river and then lean it against a picnic table. I sit down and just look out over the river. Everything is
murky and bleak, just like me. I wish that this gloomy scene could
just absorb me into itself. That I could melt down and become one
with the river and the clouds and the somber dampness that wraps
itself around me. I can feel the wetness of the damp picnic bench
soaking into my jeans and I imagine that I am growing cold and wet
and soon I will cease to exist.

But like a bad omen, the sun breaks through the clouds up
ahead. Just enough to remind me of things like warmth and

light . . . things that feel so foreign to my life right now. I squint my eyes and look away. I don't want any stupid sunshine.

I feel like a bad train wreck. Everything in me is all piled up and twisted and it can never be straightened out again. I'm certain that nothing will ever make sense again and I wonder how it can be worth the effort to just keep going. Really, what is the point? And as if the mess of my own life is not enough, I am also feeling guilty for ratting on Seth and Grace. I really don't want to go home. I'm sure they're going to call or come over and I'm sure that they'll get seriously mad at me. It's like I can't do anything right anymore. I can't live right and I don't even know how to pull off a good suicide pact without caving into the police as soon as they start pressing. I am really pathetic.

As I look out over the grayness of the water flowing swiftly in front of me, I remember how Jason and I once floated inner tubes down this very same river. Only it was sparkling and blue back then. Like an entirely different river. An entirely different lifetime. We only floated it that one time, and that was because we were bored and looking for an adventure. I think we were about thirteen that summer. Life seemed so simple back then. I don't know why things have to change so much, why people have to grow up and get so messed up that they want to kill themselves. Because, despite my own hopelessness, I still don't get it. I still don't know why Jason wanted to end his life. He seemed so much more together than the rest of us. It hurts my head to even think about it. It's like nothing makes sense anymore. And nothing will ever make sense again. I look up to see someone walking across the railroad bridge. And as I stare at this person, I begin to wonder if he or she is going out to the center to jump. Of course, I know that kids walk across the bridge sometimes, just to be daring. Jason and I even did it once, the same summer that we floated, I think. At the time I really thought I was going to have a heart attack before we finally made it across. And I swore I'd never do that again.

As the bridge-walker gets closer to my side of the river, I can tell it's a guy. I wonder if he's depressed, or if he knew Jason, or if he's going to stop any second now and take the big plunge right above the rapids that are littered with large rocks and boulders that could actually do some serious damage, if not kill him. And then I start to wonder if that guy up there might actually be Seth Blum. And now my heart is pounding and I'm about to stand up and wave my arms and tell him not to do it. In fact, I am already on my feet.

But then I see that this guy's not wearing black, and he looks shorter and stockier than Seth. And before long, he makes it all the way across the bridge and then just keeps on going. I guess I got all worried for nothing. And I feel surprised that I actually cared. I didn't think I was capable of feeling anything at all. But this incident is a vivid reminder of Seth, and Grace too, and thinking about them makes me very uncomfortable. I know that I can't hide out forever. Even so, I don't know what to do about it. Maybe the only way to fix this mess is to go directly to them and confess my stupidity. I can tell them I'm sorry for caving like that and that I'm ready to end it all now. Maybe we should take care of everything before the funeral, that is, if Seth is still pushing for it. Because, seriously, how can I go on like this? How can I last another day? Another hour? It feels so impossible.

Suddenly it's like I can't take care of this fast enough. I hop on my bike and pedal uphill, across the wet grass, over to the group picnic area. I know there's a phone booth beneath the shelter there. I'm almost out of breath as I pick up the gritty pay phone, deposit some coins, then dial Grace's home number. My heart is pounding in my ears when I hear her voice on the other end. And man, is she angry!

"Why did you do that, Morgan?" she demands. "Why did you go and turn us in to the police?"

"It was my grandma who called—"

"You told your grandma?"

"No, not everything. Just a little, and then she called the police while I was asleep and—"

"We trusted you, Morgan. And you ratted on us."

"I was worried—"

"Why didn't you call *me* first? A little warning would've been nice, you know. At least Seth did that."

"The detective kept pressuring me—"

"Well, now everyone's getting pressured. You got both Seth and me into a lot of freaking trouble—"

"I'm sorry, Grace, I didn't know what to—"

"Yeah, well thanks a lot!" she snaps and then hangs up with a loud bang.

I figure I might as well get it over with, so I put in more coins and dial Seth's number. Of course, he's nearly as angry as Grace.

"Why did you have to say anything?" he asks. "I mean, fine, if you didn't want to do it. But you didn't have to call the police and give them our names."

"I didn't actually call the police," I tell him, quickly explaining.

"What's done is done," he says in a hopeless voice.

"I'm really sorry, Seth. I was just feeling so freaked out last night. Our whole plan had fallen apart, and I was all alone in the house, and I just kind of spilled the beans to my grandma. I didn't know she'd actually call the cops."

"Yeah? Well she did."

I keep telling him that I'm sorry and that I was worried about him and finally he tells me that he and Grace just denied everything to their parents and the police.

"You're kidding?" I say. "You denied the whole suicide pact?"

"Yeah, fortunately the detective called me first, and I denied everything. Then I hung up and speed-dialed Grace's cell and tipped her off so she could do the same."

"You guys both lied to the police?"

"Morgan . . ." I can hear exasperation in his voice now. "Did you really think we'd admit to anything? How dumb is that?"

"I . . . uh . . . I don't know. I guess I'm pretty stupid then."

His voice softens now. "You were just scared. And under the circumstances, I guess we can't really blame you."

"Well, Grace sure does," I tell him.

"Yeah, she was pretty mad. But that's just because her dad was really upset."

"I totally blew it."

"Well, I should probably tell you the rest of it," he continues. "Grace actually told the police that you were the one who was trying to get the suicide pact going in the first place."

"Are you serious?"

He kind of laughs. "Yeah, I guess it was her way of getting back at you. But now the police probably think it was all your idea and that we were only at your house to try to talk you out of it."

"Great," I say. "Thanks a lot."

"Sorry," he says, "but Grace thought you deserved that much."

I groan. "Now what am I supposed to do?"

"I don't know. But I'm seriously thinking about doing this thing sooner. I told Grace that Jason's funeral seems too far out there to me. I'm thinking, why wait? Especially seeing how the heat is on now."

"And that's all my fault . . ."

"There's no point in beating yourself up, Morgan. The question is, are you still with us or not?"

"I think so." I take in a deep breath. "I mean, I'm really confused, Seth. Like sometimes I feel absolutely certain that I want this to be over with. I want everything to end, right here and now. You know?"

"Yeah, believe me, I know."

"But then sometimes I'm not so sure that I can really do it."

"Well, it'll be easier to do this together. So if you're really in, just call me. But don't wait too late."

"Too late?"

"You know . . . like I might not be around tomorrow."

I feel a chill run through me. "What about Grace?"

"Well, after her dad got mad at her, she said she wished we'd done it last night. Anyway, she and I are going to get together later on to talk about it some more."

"Where at?"

Now there is a long pause. "Look, Morgan, I really want to trust you . . . but after what happened this morning, well, I'm not so sure. In fact, I'm getting a little concerned about this conversation right now."

"I said I'm sorry, Seth. I meant it."

"Yeah, I know. How about I call you later and we can meet and talk about this some more?"

"Okay."

And then we hang up and I wonder how something as simple as killing yourself can get so complicated. I look up at the railroad bridge and think how easy it would be to go up there and just take the plunge. I even walk my bike over to a path that cuts up to the bridge overhead. It's starting to rain as I set my bike aside and climb up the muddy path that ends right next to the bridge.

I pause to catch my breath as I stand there looking at the rust-colored metal structure and then down at the gray rushing river below. Large raindrops splat down on my head and I am beginning to shiver from the damp coldness that surrounds me on all sides. I look down at the swirling rapids, rushing this way and that around the large boulders and rocks. Very wet and very cold. Then, to my surprise, I realize that I don't like the idea of getting any wetter, so I hop on my bike and pedal toward home. Even so, I am soaked by the time I get there.

"Get caught in the rain?" asks Grandma as I come inside.

"Yeah." I avoid looking at her. "I'm going to go dry off."

"How are you doing?" she asks as I head down the hallway.

I pause. "What do you mean?"

"You know what I mean, Morgan."

I feel slightly exasperated now. I mean, as much as I love Grandma, I'm still a little irritated that she called the police and got me in trouble with my friends.

"How are you feeling?" she asks again.

I turn and look at her. "I'm feeling cold and wet and like I have a serious headache," I tell her, which happens to be true.

"And that's all?"

"I don't know what you want me to say." I close my eyes now and just press my hands against both sides of my aching head. "It's like I can't even think right now. And my head feels like it's splitting open at the moment."

"Where's your Tylenol?" she asks suddenly.

"In my bedroom."

So she marches in front of me, heading straight to my bedroom, where she confiscates the whole bottle. Then she goes to the medicine cabinet in the bathroom and removes the Advil and the cough syrup and even the package of chocolate-flavored Ex-Lax.

"I'll take care of these things for the time being," she tells me.

"What about my head?" I ask.

"Here," she says as she shakes out two Advil tablets. "That should take care of it."

"Thanks a lot."

"Your friend Carlie called," she says as she walks away. "Said she's going to drop by a little later."

"Yeah, whatever." I go in my room and close the door behind me. Carlie is about the last person I want to see right now.

I've just put on dry clothes and have a towel wrapped around my head when I hear a tapping on my door. "Who is it?" I ask.

"It's me," says a female voice that I recognize. "Carlie. Can I come in?"

"Yeah, sure," I say, muttering a sarcastic *why not?* to myself.

"Hey, Morgan," she says as she comes in and looks around my abnormally neat room. "Cleaning up in here?"

I just roll my eyes as I flop down on my bed.

"So, how's it going?" she asks as she pulls out the chair by my desk.

"It's been better," I say without looking at her.

"I'm sorry I've been such a rotten friend," she says in a sober voice.

This makes me sit up and study her more closely. "Really?"

She nods. "Yeah. I've been feeling really bad. I mean, even if you did walk away from God, it wasn't right for me to walk away from you. Honestly, I'm sorry, Morgan. Will you forgive me?"

I kind of frown now. I wasn't expecting something like this from her. I mean, it was almost easier when she was acting like a jerk and I could just be mad at her. "Yeah," I finally say. "I guess I forgive you."

She looks disappointed. "You guess?"

I shrug. "Yeah, whatever."

"Okay, maybe I deserve that."

"It's not you, Carlie," I say. "It's just that I've got a lot on my mind, you know." I don't mention that I'm trying to decide whether I still want to kill myself or not. Somehow I just don't think she'd get that.

"Anyway, I came over to invite you to youth group and — "

"Forget it," I tell her.

"No, you have to listen to me," she insists. "Marcus and Tracie sent me over here — kind of like a mission — and they aren't going to take no for an answer. They said — "

"Look, Carlie," I say. "It's not like you can force me to go to youth group, you know. I have a choice in the matter and — "

"Please, Morgan!" And now Carlie literally gets down on her knees. "I'm begging you, please, come. Marcus said that it's vital for you to be there."

I just shake my head. "What is this? Some kind of spiritual intervention? You guys plan to circle around me, put your hands on me, and pray, or something weird like that?"

She laughs. "No, nothing like that. Marcus said to tell you that he has a message that he knows you need to hear."

I sigh deeply. "But maybe I can't hear it," I tell her. "I went to church with my grandma today. She forced me into that too, and I didn't hear a single word. I might as well have been asleep." Or dead.

"But Marcus said that his message has to do with Jason," she says now. And I can tell by her eyes that she thinks she's bringing out the big guns now. "He says that this is a message that he thinks Jason has given to him."

"Given to him?" I study her, wondering if this is some kind of evangelist's trick. "What do you mean?"

"I'm not really sure. But that's what he said, Morgan. I swear that's the truth."

"But you don't swear, Carlie," I remind her.

"You know what I mean," she insists.

Okay, I have to admit that she's got me curious now. Even so, I'm not convinced that it's not some kind of trick to get me back into youth group. Although I cannot imagine Marcus or Tracie pulling a cheap stunt like this. It's not their style.

"So, how about it?" she asks. "Will you come?"

"I don't know . . ."

"I'll pick you up," she says.

"But I'm not—"

"Please," she says. "Can't you just do this for Jason?"

Well, that gets me, and so I agree. "But I've got to take care of some stuff first," I tell her, glancing at the door. *Hint, hint, it's time for you to split.* Luckily she gets it and I don't have to throw her out.

"I'll be here a little before seven," she says before she leaves.

fourteen

AFTER I HEAR GRANDMA GO OUT—I ASSUME TO HER MOTOR HOME—I slip out to the kitchen and get the cordless phone and then go back into my bedroom. Then I call Seth.

"Hey," he says. "How's it going?"

I sigh. "You know, not so great."

"Yeah, I hear ya."

"Anyway, I wanted to see what you guys were planning tonight."

"Does this mean you're still in?"

"Maybe."

Long pause. He's questioning my trustworthiness.

"It's like this, Seth," I explain. "I have to go to youth group tonight—"

"Youth group?" he sounds incredulous. "Seriously? You're going to youth group?"

"It has to do with Jason—"

"*Jason?*"

"Yeah. You know that Jason was pretty involved in youth group. Anyway, the pastor, Marcus Nickerson, has some kind of message—something to do with Jason that he thinks I should hear. So I agreed."

"Oh." I can hear the disappointment in his voice.

"Hey, do you want to come?" I ask suddenly. "I mean, if it has to do with Jason—"

"No thanks, Morgan. I tried that scene once. Didn't work for me."

"Yeah, whatever. The truth is, I'm not real thrilled to be going myself. But I agreed."

"So does this mean you're out?"

"No," I tell him. "That's why I'm calling. I wanted to know if I could meet up with you guys later."

Another long pause.

"Grace isn't sure that we can trust you," he finally says.

"I know . . ." I say slowly. "And I don't blame her. But really, I'm sorry about what happened today. And if it makes you feel any better, I'm probably going to be the one who takes most of the heat, considering what Grace told the detective. Who knows, they may have surveillance watching me right now." I stand up and peer out my window, but I don't notice anything unusual.

Seth kind of laughs. "Well, okay. How about if you call Grace's cell phone after you get done with *youth group*." The way he says "youth group" sounds like he's describing something really disgusting and I can't help but think maybe he's right. Then he gives me Grace's number, which I write down on the palm of my hand, just to be safe. Then we hang up.

It's five o'clock, but I feel so exhausted that I think maybe I can actually sleep. So I lie down and before I know it Carlie is standing in my bedroom, shaking me by the shoulder and telling me it's time to get up.

"Huh?"

She smiles. "Come on, lazybones, you promised me you'd go to youth group tonight."

Somehow I manage to drag myself out of sleep and bed, and I climb into Carlie's car and listen to her chatter about mostly nothing as she drives. And I wonder what I've gotten myself into.

As we walk toward the church, I check my palm to be sure that Grace's number is still there. Although faded, it's legible. For some reason it feels like that phone number might be my lifeline. Or maybe it's my deathline. Who knows?

I insist on sitting in the back of the room, and fortunately Carlie doesn't argue. I guess she realizes that I'm only just barely here anyway. Why push her luck? I slump down and lean back in the chair, pretending to be asleep (and in truth still feeling wiped), as the worship team leads us in some "rousing" songs. Then Marcus makes some announcements about a car wash and something else that basically goes in one ear and out the other. Then, as usual, he opens the evening with a prayer, which I also manage to block out. For a moment I wonder if I might possibly be going deaf. It's like I've recently acquired this amazing ability to hear absolutely nothing.

But suddenly everything changes and I feel myself sitting upright in my seat. It's almost as if my ears have literally popped open so that I can clearly hear what Marcus is saying.

"Jesus said that we have to kill ourselves to follow him," he says for what I sense is the second time, and now the room is so quiet that I wonder if everyone is holding their breath.

"We have to *commit suicide* to find Jesus," he continues without appearing the slightest bit troubled by his disturbing words. He adjusts his small dark-framed glasses and looks around the room. "Not physical suicide, but spiritual suicide," he says, pausing again. "But then a spiritual suicide is a lot harder than a physical one anyway."

For some reason I feel like he's staring right at me, but then he looks down and opens the Bible and begins to read, he tells us, "from Matthew 16:24."

He reads, "If anyone desires to come after Me, let him deny himself, and *take up his cross*, and follow Me." He pauses and looks at us again. "Don't kid yourselves. Jesus is talking about dying. Plain and simple. To take up your cross is like saying take up your electric chair, or your hangman's noose, or your lethal injection, or even your Tylenol. I know it sounds horrible, especially in light of what we've been through over Jason's death. And I'm not trying to make light of it at all. But I think there's a message we all need to hear. I think it's what Jason would want."

I feel pretty confused now. I actually wonder if Marcus is encouraging us toward committing suicide, like maybe he plans on starting some weird cult or even a youth group suicide pact. Okay, I know this is totally ridiculous. But he does have my attention.

"I believe that our God is a great redeemer," he says. "And I believe he wants to take what Satan meant for evil and use it for good." He pauses again and almost smiles. "But I can see by your worried faces that I have some explaining to do.

"Jesus wasn't suggesting that we physically kill ourselves. But like I said, physical suicide is actually easier than a spiritual one. You see, physical death is only a momentary thing. It happens and it's done. But the kind of spiritual death that Jesus was talking about is something we must choose to do every day."

He pauses again. "I can see the confusion on some of your faces now. You want to know, *How do I kill myself on a daily basis?*"

Then he reads some more verses about how we will lose our lives if we try to hold onto them and how we will find our lives when we're willing to give up everything for Jesus' sake. And although I have read those very same verses before, they seem to be making more sense tonight. It's weird. Despite my resistance to being here, despite the fact that I'd rather be dead, it's like I am getting this.

But at the same time I don't want to.

"What good does it do if you get everything you think you want from this life?" he continues in a strong voice. "I mean, seriously, guys, even if you find your soul mate and have good friends and a cool home and a great car and even win the lottery, whatever . . . what good is it if you ultimately lose your own soul in the process? What good are those things then?"

I am leaning forward now, taking in each word as if I am starving and they are food. And maybe they are. Or not, who can know?

"But when we give all that up," he says, "when we lay all of our earthly valuables at Jesus' feet, and when we tell him that he is worth far more than all we thought we desired, that's when we truly find ourselves, because that's when we really die to ourselves. And that's when we have *real life*—the kind of life that no one can take from us—eternal life. For it's only when we die to ourselves that we find true fulfillment in Jesus."

As he continues to speak, I think about my decision to give up on faith and walk away from God. And now I wonder if I might've gotten it all backward. I mean, I really did think that God was supposed to make my life better. That he was supposed to give me what I wanted, to remake my family into one that I liked, to give me what I thought I needed. And when those things didn't happen the way I wanted them to, it's like I threw a little tizzy fit and then threw in the towel. It just didn't seem fair!

Now Marcus is inviting us to pray with him. Only I'm not sure I want to take this step. Oh, sure, a small part of me does. But another larger part has really cold feet. Besides, it's not like I can keep going back and forth like this. Like one day I'm for God and the next I'm not and then I think I can come crawling back whenever I want. It just feels wrong and false—hypocritical even. Just plain flaky. So, while the heads are bowed and no one is looking, I quietly stand up and slip out a side door.

I go downstairs, down past the bathrooms next to the sanctuary, where I know a phone is—one that is free for anyone to use as long as you're not calling long distance.

I look at the faded number on my palm and quickly dial, waiting impatiently until Grace finally answers. I tell her who it is and she says, "Oh, it's you" in that tone of voice that sounds like she wishes it wasn't.

"Grace, I'm really sorry," I begin all over again. "I already told Seth and—"

"Yeah, yeah," she says quickly. "He told me all about your apology. I'm just not sure that I buy it."

"I didn't know what to do," I tell her. "It's like the cop was sitting there right in my kitchen and just grilling me, you know, with my grandma looking on and everything. I just kinda fell apart, you know. I'm really sorry."

"Okay."

"So, where are you guys?" I ask, glancing over my shoulder at the sound of voices coming down the stairwell. They must be singing a few songs before they break up. I'm sure Carlie must've noticed I'm missing by now. I hope she doesn't come looking.

"I don't know where Seth is," she says. "But I'm at Starbucks getting a caffeine buzz like you wouldn't believe." She laughs.

"Can I meet you there?" I ask, hearing the pathetic, pleading tone in my voice.

"Yeah, I guess. Why not?"

So I quickly hang up and shoot out of the church before anyone comes to hunt me down. Fortunately Starbucks isn't that far from the church and I jog the few blocks and find Grace, like she said, slugging down a double espresso—apparently her third—when I get there.

"Man," I tell her. "You're going to be wired."

"Might as well go down shouting," she says.

"So, is this the real thing?" I ask nervously. "Are we really doing it tonight?"

She shrugs. "Well, I thought we were. Although I'll admit I've had some reservations today. That's what happens when you postpone something. It gives you too much time to think."

"So you're having second thoughts?"

She narrows her eyes at me. "Yeah, maybe."

"But you're still planning to meet Seth tonight?"

She glances around the coffee house and then rolls her eyes dramatically. "You don't see him anywhere around here, do you?"

"He's meeting you here?"

"That was the big plan."

"Oh."

She looks at her watch. "And he's like an hour late now."

"Have you tried calling him?"

She shakes her head, then finishes off the last of her espresso. "Come on," she says. "Let's go."

So I follow her out to her car and she starts driving without saying anything.

"Where are we going?"

She shrugs. "I don't know. I was just getting sick of Starbucks."

"Do you want me to call Seth?" I offer as she turns down Main Street.

"I don't know. I don't know . . ." And then she pulls over and leans her head against the steering wheel and starts to cry. "I just don't know anything anymore. I mean, it's all so hopeless and useless and, really, what's the point?"

I consider this and quietly say, "I'm not sure."

Then she sits up and looks at me by the light of the streetlamp. "Tell me the truth, Morgan. Are you really going to go through with this?"

"I don't know." I look down the street and see a patrol car coming toward us. "Grace," I whisper as if I think the patrolman can hear me. "There's a cop coming. Do you think we should go?"

"Yeah," she snaps. "Now that you've informed half the town of our little plan. They probably have an APB out on my car by now." She puts it in gear and takes off.

"I said that I'm sorry."

"What exactly are you sorry for?" she demands.

"For getting you into trouble with your dad," I say. "As lame as this sounds, I was worried about both you and Seth. Maybe I was having second thoughts too."

"But you're not now?"

"I don't know."

Grace reaches into her bag for her phone, checking to make sure it's turned on. Then she swears. "Where is he? Why hasn't he called?"

"Do you want to drive by his house?" I ask, knowing this is probably a bad idea.

"Yeah. Let's do that."

And so she drives past the street that my house is on, and, feeling guilty for leaving Grandma home alone, I glance that way and notice that my mom's little Nissan is parked right in front. So they're back. The happy newlyweds are home sweet home. Of course, this doesn't motivate me to go home. Not in the least.

Grace drives on up the hill and parks just a block away from where the Blum and Harding houses are located. We get out and walk from there.

"I don't see his car," I whisper when we get close enough to look into the carport.

"Maybe it's in the garage," she suggests.

"It's usually in the carport," I tell her. But then I realize she's not even looking at Seth's house. She's standing with her back to the rock retaining wall and looking up at Jason's house. Mostly the house looks dark. Other than the master bedroom window, which has only a faint amount of light coming through it.

"I just wish he hadn't done it," she says.

"Me too."

She sighs and leans her head back to look up. I follow her gaze to see that the clouds from today's earlier rainstorm have cleared and the stars are just becoming visible. "Do you think he's up there?" she whispers.

"Maybe."

"I want to join him," she says, her voice suddenly full of conviction. "I want to go tonight."

I consider this and find myself inexplicably thinking I should talk her into waiting. I have no idea why. I mean, why not just do this thing? Just get it over with? But here I am putting the brakes on again. "What about your idea to wait for the funeral? Don't you think that we should be there for him on Tuesday?"

She runs a hand through her thick hair and then swears again. "I don't know, Morgan! How am I supposed to have all the answers? And where is Seth anyway?"

"I don't know, but I'm thinking that maybe tonight isn't the night. I don't even know why. Maybe Jason is trying to tell us something."

"What do you mean?"

"Like maybe he wants us to stick around long enough to go to his funeral."

She reaches into her bag for a pack of cigarettes and I realize that I'm tired and cold and I just want to go home. Okay, so maybe Mom and Lover Boy are there, but all I want is to go to my own room and my own bed and just go to sleep. I wish I could sleep forever.

"I'm going to go home," I tell her as she lights up.

"Yeah, whatever."

"You going to be okay?" I ask.

She shrugs. "Oh yeah, I'm just peachy."

Now I don't know what to say. And so I just say goodbye, then trudge down the hill toward my house.

fifteen

I HAVE NO IDEA WHAT TO EXPECT AS I WALK THROUGH MY OWN FRONT door. It's entirely possible that Grandma has spilled the beans about the suicide pact and my mom could be very upset. Or maybe Bradley will play the role of "dad" and give me a lecture or even try to ground me or something as pathetic as that. But I almost don't care. I walk into the living room and see Mom's overnight bag on the floor by the hallway.

"Is that you, Morgan?" I hear her voice calling from the kitchen.

"Where's Bradley?" I ask without even greeting her. I stick my head in the doorway and look around. "Where's the happy groom?"

"Don't ask," she says in her grumpy voice.

"Lee Anne," calls my grandma as she comes through the back door. "Is that you?"

"Man, I thought that was her RV," says Mom in a hushed voice. She rolls her eyes and hurries toward the living room, like she thinks she can escape Grandma. "When did *she* get here anyway?"

"Yesterday," says Grandma as she comes into the living room with what appears to be a teapot, although it's hard to tell since it's covered by something that looks like a ratty ski hat.

"I just made a fresh pot of Earl Gray if anyone wants some." She is scowling at her daughter now, and despite myself, I feel kind of sorry for my mom. "I want to talk to you, young lady," Grandma says in a stern voice.

"Great," says my mom as she glances at me. "You must've told her about Bradley."

"Want me to get some cups for the tea?" I offer, ready to make a getaway.

"Sure," Mom says as she sinks down into the couch. "Might as well have tea since I know I won't be getting any sympathy."

By the time I return with three cups, my mom is practically in tears and my grandma looks somewhat pleased.

"They *didn't* get married," says my grandma.

I look at my mom. "Seriously?" I say. "You guys *didn't* get married?"

She just shakes her head as I hand her a cup and fill it for her. "Nope."

"Why not?" I ask as I sit down next to her.

Mom sips her tea, then says, "Because Bradley's a first-rate jerk."

I kind of smile at Grandma now. "Yeah," I say. "Tell me something I didn't know."

"And how did you know?" asks Mom.

"I just felt it," I tell her. "Something about him seemed kind of slimy to me."

"Yeah, well, thank goodness I figured it out before we actually tied the knot."

She goes on to tell us that they'd just checked into their hotel room and she'd gone to take a shower and when she came out, she overheard him talking on the phone.

"Here we were, planning to get married that night, and I discover him sitting there talking to some old girlfriend. He'd seen her in the lobby while I was registering, paying for our stupid room on *my* Visa card. Apparently this chick lives in Vegas and he thought she was married, but she'd just gotten divorced, and I think he actually wanted to hook up with her while we were there."

"Jerk!" says Grandma.

"Moron!" I add.

"Idiot," says Mom. "Well, we had a big ol' fight and I threw him out."

"But why didn't you come back?" I ask, suddenly realizing how much that could've changed things for me. "Why didn't you just come back home on that same night?"

"Oh, they don't give refunds and the room was paid for through the weekend, and I figured I deserved a little break after what Bradley put me through."

Grandma makes her tsk-tsk sound and shakes her head. Her expression is clearly one of disapproval.

"Well, why not?" demands my mom. "I should be entitled to a couple of days of—"

"Not while your daughter is dealing with a good friend's suicide at home all alone."

Now my mom's eyes get really huge and she turns and looks at me. *"What?"*

So I tell her all about Jason and she is even more shocked. And for some reason it makes me feel better to see that she's actually crying. Then she puts her arms around me and holds me tight, the way she used to when I was little. And then we are both crying together.

"I am so sorry, baby," she says as she strokes my hair. "So, so sorry. Man, I am the worst mother in the whole world."

"No, you're not, Mom," I say as we pull apart and Grandma hands each of us a Kleenex. "But your timing's not so great."

"I'll say," says Grandma. "Good thing that mine was better. Of course, I have the Lord to thank for that."

"The *Lord*?" Mom turns and stares at Grandma like she's just stepped into the twilight zone. "What?"

"I found Jesus," says Grandma. "Or rather he found me. I wanted to come home and tell my granddaughter all about it, and when I got here, I found out about the suicide pact."

"*Suicide pact?*" Now my mom turns back to me. "How many people are you talking about?"

"Two of my friends were here," I explain quickly. "They were so bummed about Jason that they wanted to kill themselves."

"And you too?" asks my mom.

I sigh and look away. "I don't know . . ."

"Morgan has put that nonsense behind her," says Grandma.

"What were the others going to do?" asks my mom. "Please, tell me there wasn't a gun involved."

"Tylenol," says my grandma, just shaking her head. "They were going to use Tylenol, Lee Anne."

Now Mom looks even more confused. "Tylenol? How can that kill you?"

"It's what Jason used," I inform her. "A lethal overdose."

"Oh."

"It seems like a simple way to go," I say as if I'm talking about how to program a DVD player. "You know, take some pills, go to sleep, never wake up . . ."

"Oh, Morgan!" Then she hugs me again. "Please, tell me that you won't ever do anything like that!"

I don't answer.

"I don't think you need to be too worried," Grandma reassures her. "Morgan talked to a policeman this morning, and then she went to church with me and then to youth group tonight." She smiles as if the world is rotating properly on its axis now. "I think God has things under control."

Mom doesn't look too sure. "I had wondered why you quit going to church."

"Well, like Grandma said, I started back up again today." Now I try to imitate my grandma by plastering this smile across my face, but it doesn't feel very convincing.

"Wow." My mom sighs. "I feel like I've been gone for a year. So much can happen in just a couple of days."

"Especially when you're not paying attention," Grandma reminds her. "Morgan might be seventeen, but she still needs her mother, Lee Anne."

"I can see that." Mom looks around the living room now. "Looks like someone cleaned the place up. Thanks, Mom."

"It wasn't me." Grandma nods in my direction.

"Oh, thanks, Morgan."

"I just needed something to keep me busy. Keep my mind off Jason, you know."

"It's so unbelievably tragic, Morgan. Jason was the sweetest kid." Then she makes a sad face. "Have you heard from your brother lately?"

I just shake my head.

"Maybe no news is good news?" she tries.

"Maybe." I finish my tea and start to leave.

"Morgan," says my mom. "I'm really sorry about all this. And I know it must be hard on you to lose Jason." She blows her nose. "He was a good kid. I just can't believe he'd do something like that."

"I know. It's pretty confusing."

"How are your other friends?" she asks. "You said there are two of them that were considering this. Are they okay now?"

I shrug. "I think so."

"Morgan's done everything she can," says Grandma. "The police and the kids' parents know what's going on now."

"Who are they?" asks Mom. "Anyone I know?"

I figure there's no point in keeping this information from my mom, especially since Grandma and the police already know. So I tell her. "Seth Blum and Grace Benson."

"You mean the Blums that live by the Hardings?" she asks.

"Yeah."

"I know Ruth Blum. She used to work at the bank. She's never seemed like the sharpest crayon in the box. Although she did marry well."

"I haven't talked to Seth since earlier today," I tell her. "But he sounded okay." Yeah, I know it's a lie. But what am I going to say? That Seth is still planning something?

"Who's Grace Benson?" asks Mom. "I don't recall that name."

"She used to date Jason. She's like one of the prettiest girls in school. She's biracial, and I guess life hasn't been that easy for her. Jason used to tell me things about her family that weren't too happy."

"I'll bet her mom is Cindy Taylor," says Mom suddenly. "I went to school with her and she married a black guy named Nick Benson. I met him once. He seemed like a really nice guy too."

"Well, he's pretty mad at Grace," I tell her.

"Morgan?" Now I can feel her eyes peering at me with that motherly stare that used to work a lot better when I was little. "Are you sure I shouldn't be worried about you?"

"Look," I tell her. "I'm fine. It's not like I'm planning on doing myself in tonight. Okay?"

"What about tomorrow?" she asks with a worried frown.

"Can anyone promise anything for tomorrow?" I say, hoping to sound wise and philosophical.

"I'm serious, Morgan."

"Oh, Mom, I'm doing the best I can, okay? If you want me to lie I could tell you that I've got everything all figured out and I know for a fact that I have absolutely no intention of killing myself today or ever. Would that make you happy?"

"I'd prefer honesty."

"Well, honestly, I'm really tired. Okay? And I should probably call Carlie and apologize for ditching her at youth group tonight."

"You ditched her?" asks Mom.

"More important," says Grandma, "you did go to youth group, right?"

"Yes to both questions."

Grandma smiles now. "Carlie told me that your youth pastor was going to have a special message."

"Yeah, well, he did." I stand now. "And if you'll excuse me, I'll go call Carlie and maybe we'll even talk about it." Then I grab the cordless phone and take it to the privacy of my room and call Carlie. Okay, I don't really want to talk to her. I just mostly want to keep her from freaking out or calling me.

After I apologize for ditching her, she asks me how I'm doing, but she uses a voice that sounds like she really cares.

"I don't know," I tell her as I flop down on my bed. "Tired mostly."

"Wasn't Marcus' message awesome?"

"Yeah, I guess. I'm still thinking about it."

"I was talking to Micah Flanders afterward, and he seemed kind of confused by it."

"Why's that?"

"He thought Marcus was saying that it was okay for Jason to kill himself."

"Oh . . ."

"I know, it sounds weird, but Micah seemed pretty convinced that's what Marcus meant."

"Well, I can understand that. Ending it all can it seem like an easy way out of everything. I mean, if someone's thinking along those lines already."

"What do you mean?" asks Carlie in an alarmed voice. "You don't really think it was okay for Jason to kill himself, do you?"

"I don't know."

"But it's wrong," she insists. "Suicide is wrong."

"Yeah, whatever."

"Seriously, Morgan, you don't really believe it's okay to kill yourself, do you?"

"I'm not sure . . . I'm not sure about much of anything anymore, Carlie."

"But you have to know that God doesn't want us to—"

"Look," I interrupt what is sounding a lot like the beginning of a sermon. "Sometimes there is more than one answer to a question. And unless you're walking in someone else's shoes, well, maybe you shouldn't try to answer it for them."

"But you would never—"

"How do you know?" Now I guess I'm just tired or stupid or whatever. Or maybe I just want to shock my conservative friend. But I spill the beans. I tell about her all about our little suicide pact. Without going into all the details, I tell her how we had it all worked out, how we were about to check out on Saturday night. "Sweet and simple—the end," I finish as if I've just ended a bed-time story.

"No way!" she says.

"Way," I reply in this offhand tone, like, hey, it's no big deal. "If my grandma hadn't come home when she did . . ." The severity of this fact actually hits me. "Well, there would've been three corpses in my mom's living room."

"No way!"

"Sad but true," I continue, but I'm thinking maybe it really is. Sad, I mean.

"So have you decided not to then?"

I consider this, and although I hate to lie to a friend, I'm just not sure that I can face a sermon from her. "Yeah, pretty much so," I tell her.

"Well, that's a relief. How about the others?"

"To be honest, I'm not totally sure. I talked to one of them tonight, but the other guy is missing."

"This is so bizarre, Morgan."

"Yeah, I guess."

"Can you tell me who they are?" she asks. "I mean, just so that I can be praying for them tonight? Especially the guy who is missing."

My first response is to refuse. But then I realize that the police know all this by now anyway and, like Grace said, probably "half the town" too. So I decide it's no biggie and just tell her.

"Wow, that's so sad, Morgan. I mean, I don't really know them that well, but they seem like really nice people. You don't really think they'd still do it, do you?"

"I don't know." Okay, now I wish I hadn't told her. Somehow it seems wrong, like I've violated their friendship or something. Like why can't I just keep my big mouth shut? What is wrong with me anyway?

"Well, I'll really be praying for them."

I don't respond to that. I'm thinking, yeah, sure, praying really helped Jason a lot too. I mean, he was a guy who actually kept a prayer list and everything. Look where that got him.

"Let me know if there's anything else I can do to help," she says. "I feel really bad, Morgan. I mean, for being such a low-life friend this past month. And now to hear that you've actually considered killing yourself . . . wow, it just makes me so sad."

"Hey, don't beat yourself up over it," I say. "People make their own choices, right? You can't blame yourself for what others do." But even as I say this, I know that I partially blame myself for Jason. I mean, what kind of friend had I been to him?

"But really, you're better now, right?" Her voice is still concerned. "I mean, you wouldn't actually—"

"Don't worry, Carlie. Sure, I'm still sad, especially when I think about Jason. But life goes on, you know . . ." Okay, I think that sounds pretty unbelievable, not to mention shallow. But she's such an optimist that maybe she'll buy into it.

"Well, seriously, I'm really going to be praying for Seth and Grace."

Then she offers to give me a ride to school in the morning and for some reason I agree. Then we say goodbye and hang up. As irritating as Carlie can be sometimes, I realize that she's not really a bad person. For the most part she's been a good friend. And maybe it'll be some comfort to have someone to hang with at school tomorrow. If I go, that is. I still can't believe that it's possible that life can really go on like normal after something like this. I mean, how can I go to school and act like everything's normal? Like I'm interested in classes or grades or anything anymore. How do people go on after something like this? It seems impossible. And I feel certain that the pain will never go away.

sixteen

I KNOW I SHOULD PROBABLY BE DOING MY HOMEWORK RIGHT NOW. I mean, it's like almost ten o'clock and tomorrow is the start of third-quarter finals week. But how can my tired brain focus on things like history and economics? Like who cares? I mean, seriously, I could've been dead by now. Along with Seth and Grace. Who would've cared about homework then?

Seth and Grace . . . I keep trying to block those guys from my mind. It's like every time I think about them, I start feeling really freaked out. I wonder where Seth is . . . if he's even alive. And Grace too. Did they get together tonight after all? And if they did, will they pull this thing off—without me? I feel so helpless. And hopeless.

It was nice that Carlie seemed to care so much and that she said she'd pray for them. It wouldn't surprise me if she was doing that right now. Still, I can't see how it makes any difference. People do what they want to do. How can God stop them? He sure didn't stop Jason. I think about what Marcus said tonight, about how we need to kill ourselves spiritually—to commit spiritual suicide. As weird as it sounds, it still sort of makes sense to me—or at least to some part of me. I mean, it's not like my head really gets it. Maybe it's my heart that understands. And maybe Marcus is right. Maybe I do need to give *everything* up to God. I mean, I know that I've never really done that before. Oh, I believed in God, alright, but I never really gave *everything* up to him before. I wonder if I could even do that now. Or if I even want to.

Suddenly, it seems pretty clear. And it's like I have to ask myself this really hard question: Okay, if I was willing to give up *everything* by killing myself, why wouldn't I be willing to give up *everything* for God and continue to live? And as soon as I allow myself to actually consider this question, the tears start to fall and it's like I can feel God right here in my bedroom and he's tapping me on the shoulder and asking me to answer my own question. Give up everything to kill myself? Or give up everything to live for God? Why is it so difficult?

Finally I just throw up my hands and say, "Okay, God, I give up! You got me! *I do want you, and I do want your way.* Because my way totally sucks." Then I actually get down on my knees and offer my life to God again, only this time I can tell it's different. It's like I really do want to do it God's way from now on, even though I don't know exactly what that means. But if it means dying to my own selfish wants, then, okay, I think it's worth it. I think it's about time.

I stay on my knees for a long time, so long that they actually start to ache. But it's like I'm afraid to move, like I don't want this moment to end. Because, somehow, I know it is real. I know it is God. And I know that I've made some real promises here tonight. Some promises that I have to keep. God help me!

When I finally stand up my face is wet with tears. But these tears have the faint taste of hope in them.

I go back over to my dresser and I get the strong impression that it's time to put away the Jason shrine. And although it feels hard to do this, I suspect that it's God and that he's trying to make a point of some kind. So I put the T-shirt and baseball mitt and the other things into an empty box that I put up on the shelf in my closet. Then I pick up the black-and-white photos of Jason. I still want to take them to the Hardings' after school tomorrow. I know it won't be easy, but I feel like it's something I just need to do. I think they would appreciate them. And I have the negatives so I can easily make more.

But before I put the photos in an envelope, I look at Jason's face one more time. And for the first time since this whole horrible thing happened, I take my pain directly to God and ask him, *Why?* Why did Jason do this? But I don't hear an answer. I guess I didn't really expect to. I just felt like I needed to ask. And somehow I think God wanted me to ask. I think he wants me to keep the communication lines open from now on.

And, feeling guilty for having closed those lines, I tell God that I'm really sorry for turning my back on him. And I thank him for not giving up on me. And even though I don't have all the answers and I may never know why Jason did this, I tell God that I want to trust him with all these things.

I feel better as I put Jason's photos into the envelope. Of course, I still miss my friend desperately. And I don't think this dull ache deep inside of me will ever really go away. Maybe that's my own fault. Maybe this is the scar I will always bear. The price I'll pay for not having been a better friend. Because I still feel guilty for not being there for Jason. And I think that if I hadn't turned my back on God and been so obsessed with my own problems, I might've said or done something that could have prevented this.

To be honest, it's still killing me.

"I'm sorry, Jason," I whisper out loud to the last photo. "I wish I had been paying better attention. I wish I could do this whole thing all over again and do it right. I'm so sorry."

Then I tell God that I'm sorry too. And although my head knows that God forgives me, I think my heart is unconvinced.

The truth is, I don't think I can ever forgive myself. And I just don't know how a person can live with this kind of guilt. I think it could eat me alive.

Is this supposed to be part of my spiritual suicide? Is this is how I take up my cross every day? How I die to myself? Maybe I just think about how I let Jason down, how badly I blew it, and how he is gone now . . . and part of me dies.

Maybe that's not exactly what Marcus Nickerson meant tonight. I don't know for sure. Maybe it'll all make more sense in time. As Grandma said, "Rome wasn't built in a day." Yeah, duh.

I set these thoughts aside as I gather Grace's things, her Jason memorabilia, and I put it all in my backpack so I can give it to her at school tomorrow. If she goes to school, that is. I am stabbed with fresh guilt as I remember how I left her standing all alone tonight. I can still see that lost look on her face, reflecting my feelings exactly. And then I just deserted her. What kind of friend am I anyway? I mean, here I am suffering over losing Jason, and then I abandon someone who's hurting so badly that she might take her own life. What is wrong with me anyway?

Feeling desperate, I look at my palm and am relieved to see the barely legible numbers. With my heart pounding I call her cell, and then I get really concerned when it seems she's not answering. Like where is she? Finally I hear her voice and it feels like I can breathe again.

"How are you doing?" I ask.

"Not so great." Her voice sounds hoarse, like she's been crying again.

"I'm sorry," I tell her.

"Yeah, me too."

"Have you heard from Seth?"

"No."

I feel a mixture of relief and terror now. I'm relieved because Grace hasn't hooked up with Seth and gone off and killed herself. But at the same time I'm seriously frightened because I know that Seth is serious about committing suicide tonight.

"Do you think he's okay?" I ask in an unsteady voice.

"Okay?" Her tone is sarcastic. "What do you mean by okay?"

"Alive."

Long pause. Then she says, "I don't know. Does it matter?"

I consider this. "Yeah, actually I think it does matter, Grace."

"Why?" And I can tell by the way she says "why" that she really means it. So I think carefully about my answer.

"I've had a change of heart," I admit.

"Surprise, surprise." Now she sounds irritated. Like she thinks I'm bailing on her or something.

I wonder how much I want to tell her, then decide to be honest. "Look, Grace," I begin. "I've decided I want to give this God thing another chance. And I know you might not get that, but it's like I know that he doesn't want me to kill myself. It's like he wants me to die to him . . . so that I can live." Then I wish I hadn't said that much, because I'm thinking there's no way she's going to get this. I mean, I barely get it myself.

But she just says, "Huh," like she's actually thinking about it.

"And anyway," I continue carefully, "after taking a little time to think things over, I can see how it would be so wrong to kill myself. So stupid. Such a mistake."

"Why?"

"Okay . . ." I pause to gather my thoughts. "Well, for one thing, it's irreversible, Grace. I mean, think about it. Once you take your life, that's it. You don't get to change your mind. There are no retakes. You're just dead. Period. End of story."

"Yeah, I've kind of been thinking along those lines. Dying is pretty permanent, isn't it?"

"Jason's not coming back," I say.

She sighs.

"So, are you going to be okay tonight?" I ask.

"As in, I won't kill myself?"

"Yeah."

"Not tonight, Morgan. I'm too tired. I just want to go to sleep."

So I tell her to sleep well, then hang up. I'm so glad I called her. I know it doesn't make up for Jason. But it's something. And now I realize that all I can do is pray and hope that Grace finds a reason not to give up—and that she'll discover how God can help.

Once again, I try to focus on my homework, but it still seems so trivial—so stupid in light of everything else. And even though I've tried to keep my grades up this year, I'm no longer sure that I care. I mean, does it really matter if I get a scholarship or not? So what if I end up going to community college? Jason won't be going anywhere. And as much as I want to move on from this, to quit obsessing over him, it's like I'm kind of stuck. Not only that, but I am getting seriously worried about Seth now.

I keep imagining that he's doing it tonight, that he's imitating Jason and overdosing on Tylenol and everything that happened on Friday will be happening all over again by tomorrow. And I just don't think I can take it. Not only that, but this time I realize that maybe I actually have the power to stop it.

So, even though it's nearly eleven o'clock, I decide to call his house, just to make sure he isn't out doing something stupid.

Hopefully he's home doing his homework. Yeah, right.

I feel really nervous as I listen to the phone ringing. I imagine that everyone's in bed and that they're going to think I'm some kind of nutcase. A woman, I assume his mom, answers the phone and then tells me that Seth's not there.

"I'm sorry to call so late," I say quickly. "Do you happen to know where he is?"

"No, but I think he should be home soon," she says in a somewhat irritated voice, "since it's a school night."

"Well, this is Morgan Bergstrom," I say, feeling even more nervous since I'm sure she will recognize my name from the whole police-report thing.

"Morgan!" Her tone morphs into something surprisingly kind. "How are you doing?"

"Better," I tell her. "But, of course, I'm still really sad about Jason."

"Yes, we all are."

"And I'm pretty concerned about Seth."

"Oh, you mean that nonsense with the police and all. Well, you shouldn't worry about that. As long as you're feeling better, that is. I've been concerned about you and I was hoping you'd get some help."

"Thank you," I say. "But right now I'm more worried about Seth. I know you probably think I'm interfering, and I'm sure he's probably denying it, but he was *very* committed to our suicide pact. Out of the three of us, he was the most certain about wanting to go through with it. I really think he may need some help, Mrs. Blum."

"Oh, I appreciate your concern, Morgan. But I think that everything's under control now." She pauses and I suspect she thinks I'm totally clueless. "Now, you just make sure to take care of yourself and get help if you need it, dear. I was so glad to hear that your grandmother is with you now. It's too bad that you were left alone at such a difficult time. Will your mother and her new husband be back soon?"

I am amazed at how much this woman seems to know about me and my family, but it's obvious that Seth has been talking to her. And maybe that's a good sign. "My mom got back today," I tell her.

"Well, that's good. And I appreciate your concern for Seth, but he seems to be just fine now. In fact, he really seems to be improving. He's taken an interest in things like cleaning his room and getting himself more organized for school. And he's been talking to his dad and me more lately. It's sad to think that this may be the result of the Hardings' sorrows. But perhaps it's true that God can bring good out of evil."

Well, I just don't know what to say to that, so, feeling frustrated, I end our conversation and hang up.

Okay, I am really concerned about Seth now. The things his mom described sound more like what I did when I was planning on checking out than the actions of someone who's turned some kind of corner. So now I'm praying that God will somehow get to him before he does anything stupid. How about a miracle, God?

seventeen

IT'S REALLY LATE AND I KNOW I SHOULD GO TO BED, BUT AS I'M GETTING ready, I notice the bag with all the rolls of used film still on my dresser. I get this kind of sick feeling in the pit of my stomach. Okay, I know it's a small thing in light of everything else, but I was supposed to use that film for the yearbook. Then I realize that I can simply buy some replacement film with my own money from my savings. And I suppose I'll have to pay to have them developed since I'm curious to see how they turned out. Still, I cannot believe how stupid I have been the last couple of days. I guess my one consolation is that at least I'm alive. That's something.

After I turn off the lights and get into bed, I keep hearing the words of that Simon and Garfunkel song running through my head. "Hello darkness my old friend, I've come to talk to you again. . . ." It's like I'm being haunted or something.

Finally I can't take it anymore, and I have to get out of bed and just turn on a light. And then I take my Bible out of the drawer where I've managed to ignore it these past few weeks, and I open it up and begin to read.

Ironically (or maybe not), I open to John 8:12. I read the verse over and over until I have it memorized and Jesus' words finally block out the words of that depressing song.

I am the world's Light. No one who follows me stumbles around in the darkness. I provide plenty of light to live in.

***

When I wake up on Monday morning, I feel a little better, but I wouldn't say that I'm happy because I am not. Still, I feel like maybe I can face this day. Maybe.

"How you doing?" my mom asks as I drink some juice and wait for my bagel to toast.

"I feel a little better today," I tell her.

"I thought about Jason a lot last night," my mom says. "It just makes me so sad."

"Me too."

Then my mom hugs me. "I'm so glad you're okay, Morgan. And I'm so sorry I've been such a sorry excuse for a mom lately. Things are going to be changing around here."

I check out my mom's outfit. It's much more conservative than what she'd been wearing during her Bradley era. "You look nice," I tell her.

"More mom-like?"

I force a smile. "Hey, it's okay to want to look younger. I mean, as long as you don't push it too far."

"I think I was just having a little midlife crisis," she admits.

"And I was having an end-of-life crisis."

"What do you mean?"

Now I realize that I never really confessed my part of the suicide pact to her. It's like it's been my little secret. But suddenly I think I should just get it out into the open. And so I tell her.

She hugs me again. "I suspected as much, Morgan. It just didn't make sense that your friends were over here planning on killing themselves and you weren't involved. I'm just glad that it's over now."

I nod as I reach for my bagel.

But now she's peering into my eyes, almost as if she's not so sure. "It is over, isn't it?"

"Yeah, it's over for me," I say as I smear cream cheese on my bagel. I just hope that it's over for Seth and Grace too."

Mom looks out the window. "Carlie's here," she tells me.

"Gotta go," I say as I grab my bag and head out.

I finish eating my bagel as Carlie drives us the short distance to school. "Thanks for the ride," I say as she parks in the front lot. And I really am glad that she's doing this because I'm sure it'll be a lot easier going to school today with Carlie by my side. I realize once again that I really appreciate her a lot.

"I'll warn you," she says as we go through the front doors. "The kids made this kind of shrine thing at Jason's locker on Friday afternoon."

I nod. "We made a shrine for him at my house too."

"Really?"

"Yeah. For some reason it was sort of comforting."

I stop in front of Jason's old locker and just stare at all the stuff. There are flowers and photos and teddy bears and balloons. Weirdly enough, it almost looks like some sort of party or celebration.

"Kind of strange, huh?" she whispers to me.

"But it probably makes kids feel better to leave this stuff here, you know?" Even so, I feel the lump growing in my throat again, and I'm afraid I could fall apart any minute. Somehow, just seeing his locker and knowing that he's never coming back really gets to me.

"How's it going, Morgan?" Micah Flanders comes up and stands next to me in front of the locker.

"This is hard," I admit.

"Tell me about it."

I turn and look at Micah now, remembering what Carlie said about his reaction to Marcus' message at youth group last night. "How are you doing, Micah?"

"Not so good."

"We're all going to miss him."

"I don't know how you get over something like this," he says sadly.

"Have you talked to the grief counselor?" I ask.

He makes a face. "Yeah, like I want to go talk to some stranger about it."

I nod. "I know what you mean. You can talk to me if you want, Micah. I know we haven't really been friends since, well . . ." Now I'm kind of embarrassed, because we've hardly spoken to each other since last October when he and I went out together a couple of times. It had been Jason's idea, a way to double with him and Grace. But then Micah dumped me for Lanna Halston and my feelings got a little hurt.

"Morgan," he says in a lowered voice like he doesn't really want anyone else to hear, "I'm really sorry about what happened last fall."

"No problem," I say lightly. "It was just awkward, you know?"

"Friends now?" he asks, sticking out his hand as if he wants me to shake it.

I shake his hand and nod. "Friends."

He sighs. "You know, I really would like to talk to you. I know that you and Jason were close and, well . . ." He looks over his shoulder as if he wants to keep this private too. "Maybe we can talk during lunch. Okay?"

"Sure."

The first bell is ringing now and I know it's time to head to class. But I am curious as to what Micah wants to talk about. I mean, I realize it has to do with Jason. But why is he keeping it so down low?

I keep an eye out for Seth and Grace all morning, but I never see them. This is making me more worried than ever. I even ask some of their friends, but no one seems to have seen them. At lunchtime, Micah catches me in the lunch line and asks me to sit with him over on the far side of the cafeteria. And that's where he spills the beans.

"I heard about the pact," he begins.

"The pact?"

"Yeah. With you and Seth and Grace." He glances around as if he's uncomfortable. "I don't really know Seth that well and I haven't been able to get in touch with Grace. So I thought I'd talk to you."

"How did you hear about it?" I ask.

"Everybody knows."

"Seriously?"

"Well, maybe not everybody. But kids from church know. I think someone put it on the prayer chain or something."

I look across the room to where Carlie is sitting with some of our youth group friends. I'm sure she must be the one who told. Not that it matters really. If anything, I think I'm glad to know that she and I aren't the only ones praying for Seth and Grace. But I admit I'm a little embarrassed that people may still be thinking I want to kill myself.

"Yeah, we sort of had a pact," I admit to him. "But I'm not in it anymore. For that matter, I'm not sure Grace is either."

Now he looks disappointed.

"Why?" I ask him.

He just shrugs and pokes at his macaroni and cheese.

"Micah," I say in a firm voice. "Are you considering something like this yourself?"

He keeps shrugging and poking, but I know that he is.

"It's crazy, Micah," I tell him. "Sure, we're all totally depressed about Jason. And it makes absolutely no sense. But taking your own life isn't going to help anything. Can't you see it'll only make things worse? I mean, what if everyone in the school just started killing themselves?"

"Keep it down," he warns me.

"But, Micah," I continue in a quieter voice. "Please tell me that you're not really thinking about this. It's not the answer. I'll admit that I came really, really close on Saturday night. But I'm seriously thanking God today that I didn't do it. I mean, if I'd done it, that would be it. I would be dead and there would be no second chances. Do you see that?"

"All I can see is that I picked the wrong person to talk to." He's standing now.

"But *Micah*."

He waves his hand at me. "Forget about it, Morgan."

I go over to sit with Carlie now. I feel not only like a failure but also like I've played a role in getting someone like Micah to consider suicide.

"What's wrong?" asks Carlie.

I look around the table, studying the faces of the youth group kids, as I wonder how much I should say. But then they already know about this anyway.

"This whole suicide thing," I say. "It's like it won't go away. Someone just told me that he wanted into the pact. Like I'm even in the pact anymore."

"Micah?" asks Carlie.

I shrug, but I can tell she knows. "I told him that I'm not into it now and that I don't agree with it and how it's wrong and everything."

"Would he listen?" asks Matt, a senior who takes a fairly active role in the youth group.

I shake my head and look down at my unfinished lunch. I don't feel very hungry anymore.

"Well, Micah's not the only one," says Carlie in a hushed voice. "I heard that several other kids are talking about it. They want in too."

"You gotta be kidding," I say.

"Don't I wish."

"This is crazy," I tell her. "It's getting way out of hand. Is there anything we can do?"

"We're all praying," says Matt. "But I think we have a responsibility to do more than that."

"Like what?" I demand.

"Maybe we need to let someone know," he suggests.

I nod. "I agree, but trust me, it's a lot easier said than done."

"Morgan's already taken heat for telling on Seth and Grace," says Carlie.

"What if there was a way that kids could give names anonymously?" suggests Eva Fernandez.

"Yeah," I say, getting an idea. "What if there was an anonymous box where kids could put names of kids who might be thinking about killing themselves? That way no one would get in trouble for being an informant."

"That could work," says Matt.

"Yeah." I stand up now. "It could. And I'm going to the office right now to tell someone."

"I'll go with you," offers Carlie.

Before long, we are talking to the counselor and explaining how hard it is to turn in a friend who might be considering suicide and take the heat for telling.

"That's a great idea," says Mrs. English. "I'll see to it that a box is placed outside of the office as soon as possible." She looks at me. "In the meantime, do you have some names to share?"

"How about if I put them in the box," I offer.

She nods. "Yes. That's fine."

Before the end of fifth period, a small locked, wooden box appears on the counter outside the office and an announcement is made explaining why it's there. I've already made my short list, only three names, but that's more than enough. I slip it into the box and hope no one's looking.

To my surprise I notice a couple of other kids slipping names into the box as well. I'm curious what names are going in and even wonder if someone might be writing mine down, since the rumor is still circulating about our original pact. But I decide that I won't worry about that for now. Mostly I just want Seth, Grace, and Micah to get help. And anyone else who is thinking about taking "the easy way out." Yeah, right.

eighteen

BECAUSE I WENT HOME EARLY ON FRIDAY, I NEVER SAW THE SCHOOL PAPER last week. But I pick up a copy in my journalism class and absently thumb through it as Mr. Spencer talks about some new software that he plans to have up and running after spring break. Mostly the paper reads like yesterday's news. But then I come to the editorial section and, seeing Jason's usual smiling photo above his regular column, I stop and just stare. I can see that his column is shorter than usual, but I'm curious. So I read.

WHY CAN'T WE?
Jason Harding

When are we going to figure it out? When are we going to accept that everyone is different — and that it's a good thing? I am so sick and tired of trying to fit in, trying to live up to what someone else's image of me is, trying to become what someone else thinks I should be. What is wrong with just being me?

What has happened to our society in this "new and improved" millennium? Have we evolved into a cookie-cutter culture where everyone must look and act and walk and talk the same in order to be accepted? Whatever happened to diversity? To *viva la difference*?

Why can't we just be ourselves? And why can't we just accept each other for who we are and then get on with it? I mean, do we really want to live in a world where everyone is the same? Seriously, people, how much more boring can it get?

And yet I saw the same stuff going on just this week. Kids picking on kids — and why?—because someone is different. Because someone is daring to be unique. Brave enough to stand up against the norm. And then he gets shot down. Just like that.

Man, I just don't get it. Why can't we figure it out before it's too late? Why can't we?

I close the paper and sigh. I can hear Jason's voice in my head now. I can hear him asking those questions and demanding some answers. They're just the kinds of questions he liked to ask. He liked to make kids think, liked to challenge others to stretch themselves. Who will do that now?

I get an extra copy of the paper as I'm leaving class. I think I will give it to his family when I take the photos to them in case they haven't seen it yet. I don't want them to forget what kind of a guy he was. Despite what has happened, I want them to be proud of him. I want them to accept him.

The editorial reminds me of Seth. He's one of those guys who likes to buck the system and takes plenty of heat because of it. But Jason always defended him, always stuck up for him. I continue looking for Seth off and on all day, but I don't see him once. I try to reassure myself that he's probably just skipping school, but I have to admit that I'm worried it could be something worse.

I finally see Grace in the afternoon. I'm so relieved that she's here that I go straight to her and actually give her a hug, which I'm sure surprises her.

"I've got some of your things in my locker," I say as I step away. "From Jason's memorial, you know. I thought you'd want them back."

She shrugs, then looks away. "Yeah, I guess. I'll get them later."

"How are you doing?"

She sighs. "I don't know . . ."

"You're not still—"

"Don't talk about it here," she snaps.

"Sorry."

"I've already had to tell too many people that it was all a hoax." She looks over her shoulder. "It won't help matters for me to be seen talking with you."

"Okay." I step back, feeling dismissed.

"Sorry," she says. "I guess I'm just being paranoid."

"Yeah, me too, actually. This hasn't been an easy day."

"Tell me about it."

"Have you seen Seth?"

"No, but I talked to him this morning."

I feel relief ripple through me. "So he's okay then?"

"Once again, that depends on how you define okay."

"He's alive."

"Yeah, if you can call it that. Apparently he was out getting stoned last night."

"But is he still planning—"

"Why don't you call me on my cell?" she suggests. Then she gives me her number again, and for a second time I write it down on my palm.

"Hey, Grace," says Carlie as she comes up to join us.

"Hey," says Grace back. "Well, I gotta go."

"You want a ride home, Morgan?" asks Carlie as Grace heads down the hall.

"Sure. But do you think you could drop me off somewhere?"

"Yeah. Where?"

I pull the large envelope out of my bag. "I need to give these photos to Jason's mom."

"Oh." She nods as if she understands. "No problem."

"Thanks," I tell her. "Seriously."

"I need to make up for being such a lame excuse for a friend during the last few weeks," she says as she fishes her car keys from her oversized bag. "I'm glad you don't hate me."

"Life's too short to hate," I say as we go outside.

"Yeah," she agrees. "Have you noticed how everyone at school is being so nice? It's like this thing with Jason made people stop and think about something besides themselves for once. But I gotta wonder how long it'll be before kids go back to their old selves."

"Did you read Jason's column?" I ask.

"Yeah, it was great."

"He never picked on kids," I say as we get in her car.

"Jason was one in a million."

"And now he's gone."

"Yeah."

We drive in silence up to his house. I'm grateful that Carlie doesn't want to talk just now. I don't think I could take it. It's like that dull ache is just gnawing away at me again. I miss him so much. I wonder if I'll ever stop missing him—if this pain will ever end.

Once we're there, Carlie offers to stick around and give me a ride home. But I tell her that I don't mind walking, especially since it's all downhill from here anyway.

"Call me," she says. "Let me know how it goes."

I tell her that I will. Then, bracing myself, I walk up the familiar path that leads to his front door. I feel my heart beginning to race as I wait.

His mother opens the door. "Morgan?"

Her appearance surprises me. She doesn't look a bit like the Mrs. Harding that I know. Her hair, which is usually styled to model perfection, looks like she just got out of bed. And instead of her usual designer suit, she is wearing sweats. And without makeup, she looks about twenty years older.

"I'm sorry," I say quickly. "Is this a bad time? I should've called first."

She shakes her head. "No, no, it's all right. I know I look a mess, but I remember now that I told you to come by."

"Really," I say. "If this is a bad time . . ."

"No, come in. Please, come in."

The drapes are drawn and the house is quiet. And I suspect, by the pillow and blanket on the couch, that she's been sleeping in here. She quickly removes these things and invites me to sit down.

"I brought the photos," I tell her, feeling like such an intruder. I don't know why I came today. Why didn't I just wait? It's obvious that this poor woman is really suffering right now.

She reaches for a pair of glasses on the coffee table. "I'd love to see them," she says.

I remove the large envelope from my bag and take out the photos and hand them to her.

"Oh my," she says as she looks at the first one. "This is very good." Then she lays it on the coffee table and looks at the next one. One by one she goes through the small stack, laying them out like a fan across the coffee table. And then we just sit there in silence and I wonder if I should go now. Then I remember the newspaper.

"I brought you something else," I say as I pull the paper from my bag. "It's last week's paper. I thought you might like to have it." I open it up. "Jason's editorial is here. It's really good."

She takes the paper and eagerly begins reading it. And I just sit there and feel uncomfortable. Why don't I just leave? Finally she finishes it and sets it aside, then looks up at me with tears in her eyes. Now I feel criminal. Maybe I shouldn't have brought her the newspaper. Or maybe I shouldn't have come at all.

"I'm sorry," I tell her as I begin to choke up as well. "I didn't want to make you feel bad—"

"No, Morgan, don't mind me." She reaches for a handkerchief and waves her hand at me. "I do this all the time. And, really, the photos are wonderful." She picks up one of my favorites and studies it again. "You are an excellent photographer."

"Thanks."

"Do you think this one could be enlarged?"

"Sure. Of course. I can do it for you. How big do you want it?"

"They suggested having some photos of Jason for the service tomorrow. So that people can see him, you know." She leans over and picks out a couple more. "Do you think you could enlarge all of these?"

"Sure," I say. "No problem. I can do it first thing in the morning, if that's okay."

"I'll pay you, of course. For your time and materials—"

"No," I tell her. "I'd rather do it as a gift."

"You were always such a good friend to Jason." She sets the photos aside and just looks at me now, almost as if she's really seeing me for the first time. "I could never understand why you two didn't date."

"We sort of tried it once, but it kind of ruined everything. Being friends was better."

"Yes, I suppose I can understand that. Jason thought highly of you."

I swallow hard now. "I really miss him."

She nods. "I know."

"It's still hard to believe I'll never see him again."

"It is hard." She glances at the school newspaper, then looks quickly away, as if she wants to forget about it.

"And I know you must be feeling it way more than I am." I look at the dark shadows beneath her red-rimmed eyes. "I'm so sorry, Mrs. Harding."

"I'm sorry too."

I think I should probably go now. But I feel so bad for her, just sitting there, staring at the photos of Jason. She looks so lonely and lost.

"I just don't understand why he did it," I say. "Of all people, Jason seemed to have it so together." I shake my head. "I mean, my life, compared to his, has always been a real mess. It just doesn't make sense. Why would he give up like that?"

Her eyes take on a new intensity now, as if she's considering something, and then she speaks. "He didn't mean to do it, you know."

I'm not sure I've heard her right. "He didn't mean to do it?"

She shakes her head. "No. It was just a horrible mistake."

"A mistake?" Now I'm getting worried. Has this thing with Jason messed with her mind? "What do you mean?"

"I mean he didn't really want to die."

I nod as if I understand, although I'm not sure that I do. Not entirely. "You mean that if he had it all to do over again, that maybe he wouldn't have done it?"

"Exactly."

"Yes, that's what I'm trying to believe too."

"It's the truth."

Well, I'm not sure how to respond to this. In some ways she's sounding kind of weird right now. So I just nod and pretend that I understand.

"He was upset that day," she says. "He was worried about his grades and felt sure that he wasn't going to get into Princeton." She made an exasperated face. "I never cared if he went there. What difference does it make where you go to school, really?"

"I don't know." I wait for her to continue.

"He and his father argued that morning. Gary told Jason that it was up to him, that if he wanted it badly enough he should be able to pull his grades up and do what it takes to get in. 'You're a Harding,' he said—as if that really meant something." She exhales loudly, like she's attempting to blow away the pain.

"I know that Jason was concerned about college," I admit.

"Did he talk to you about that?" She seems eager for a response.

"Yeah. We talked about lots of stuff."

"Did he tell you his problems?"

Now I feel like total slime. "The truth is, I usually upstaged Jason in the problem arena." I take in a quick breath, fighting to hold off the tears. "I was probably so obsessed over my own life that I wasn't much of a listener, especially lately. Even on that day"—I choke now—"on the day that he—he did it, he had e-mailed me, saying he needed to talk. And I was so busy with my own stupid life that I never even saw the e-mail. I didn't even reply." Now the tears are coming again, fast and hard.

Mrs. Harding picks up a box of Kleenex and comes to sit beside me on the couch. She puts an arm around my shoulders. "We're all blaming ourselves, Morgan. I guess it's natural."

"I just feel so horrible about it." I wipe my nose. "Jason was always there for me. He was a great listener. And then when he really needed me, I wasn't even available."

"No one is perfect."

"I know. I just wish I could go back and do it all over again."

"So did he."

"So did *he*?" I turn to look at her face. "What do you mean? How would you even know that?" I want to ask her if Jason has been speaking to her from the grave, but that would sound disrespectful, not to mention mean.

"I haven't really told anyone all this. Well, other than Jason's father. But, as I mentioned, Jason had been down about the pressure that his father had been putting on him to get into Princeton." She nods to the school newspaper. "I wouldn't be surprised if that was part of his reason for writing that column. It had been an ongoing battle at our house."

She stands now, pacing as she continues to speak, almost as if I'm not in the room. "Jason had even said something about the pressure that very morning, something that should've clued me in, but I missed it. It was right after their big argument. He told me that everyone would probably be much happier if he wasn't around anymore. And he said that if he were gone, our family wouldn't have to be embarrassed by him anymore. Of course, I never took this seriously. Why would I?"

"People say things like that," I tell her. "But it doesn't mean they want to take their own lives."

"I certainly didn't think so at the time. Now I wish I'd been paying more attention. He came home from school around noon and seemed pretty down. He told me that he wasn't feeling well, but when I asked him for specifics, he was vague. Then he went straight to his room and turned on his music, and I really didn't think much of it. I'd ordered a bunch of flowers and had come home to get them planted that afternoon. So I went outside and worked until it was time to fix dinner. I never once thought to go check on him. Why would I?"

"You wouldn't."

"I fixed a simple dinner. His father had a council meeting and wasn't planning to get home until late. They've been working on that initiative. So it was just the two of us. But when I went upstairs to tell him to come down, he said he wasn't hungry. Well, I wasn't too pleased that I'd gone to the trouble to fix dinner and he wasn't even hungry. But I still didn't think anything was wrong with him. Not really."

I nod and wait for her to continue.

"But later on that evening, I began to feel this little thing, kind of like a nudge in the back of my head, and I felt I should go up and try to talk to him, to see if he was really sick or just feeling unhappy about the argument he'd had with his father. So I knocked on his door, and after what seemed several minutes, he told me to come in." She pauses and I can tell by her expression that she's seeing it all over again, playing it back through her mind's eye.

"But he *told* you to come in?" I repeat, wanting to make sure that I'm getting this correctly. "So he was still conscious?"

"Oh yes. He was very conscious. And agitated. I asked him if he was okay and he kind of laughed, but not in a humorous way. Then he said that he'd never felt better. And yet, I could tell by looking at him that this wasn't true. He was perspiring and shaky and his face was flushed. I told him he looked unwell. But he assured me that he was okay and that everything was going to be just fine. His music was still playing. Not so loudly, though. I suggested he get some rest. And he promised me that he would. 'Don't worry,' he said, 'I'll get lots of rest tonight.'" She reaches for her handkerchief again, blotting the tears that are slipping down her pale cheeks.

I don't know what to say, but I'm hoping she'll continue. I really feel like I need to hear all of this. And maybe she needs to tell someone.

"So I went back to my bedroom. I had the TV on and was reading a book and waiting for Gary to get home. I have a hard time going to sleep when he's not home. And it was nearly midnight when I heard someone tapping on the bedroom door. I was surprised to see that it was Jason and now he looked seriously ill. He said he was in pain, his stomach hurt horribly and he needed help. I thought perhaps he was having an appendicitis attack. My brother had suffered one when he was about the same age. So I immediately got on the phone and called 911. They asked me for his symptoms and I was trying to get him to explain it to me and he seemed confused, and then he told me that he'd taken too much Tylenol. Well, I felt kind of silly then, calling 911 because he'd taken Tylenol and gotten a tummy ache. But the woman on the other end demanded to know exactly how many pills he'd taken." She just shakes her head now, as if she can't bear to say the next words.

"I think the news said between eighty and ninety caplets," I offered.

"Yes, that's what he told me. I was so shocked at this. I had no idea why he'd do such a thing. But even so, I wasn't terribly worried. I figured Tylenol couldn't really hurt a person." She sighs. "Then the woman asked how long ago he'd taken them and Jason told me he'd taken them that morning, right after he and his dad had argued. Nearly eighteen hours earlier. I asked if I should bring him to the hospital, but she said that an ambulance was already on its way. In fact, it arrived about the same time she told me this."

Somehow this story is nothing like what I'd imagined. I had envisioned Mr. and Mrs. Harding finding Jason unconscious, then rushing him to the hospital. It strikes me as strange that he was fully aware at the time.

"Then what happened?" I ask, no longer able to be patient.

"They took him straight to the ER," she continues. "I was allowed to stay with him. But it was too late to pump his stomach. They had him on IVs and machines, but somehow I could tell by the doctor's face that it was very, very serious. That's when Jason told me that he didn't really want to die. That he'd only taken the Tylenol to shake everyone up. He figured he'd get to a certain place, then go to the hospital and have his stomach pumped. He'd only done this to show us that he couldn't take the stress and pressure anymore. He wanted to get at his dad . . . to make him understand . . ."

She chokes up, and now I put my arm around her shoulders, and I wish for something to say, something to make things better and to comfort her. But I have nothing. Mostly I am in shock. It was hard enough to hear that Jason took his own life last week. But to hear that he was sorry about it, that he regretted his choice and didn't really mean to die . . . well, this is something completely different.

"There was nothing we could do," she says. "Nothing the doctors could do. The poison from the acetaminophen was already in his system. His liver was damaged beyond repair. He died at around three in the morning. His father got there before then. But Jason was in such pain that it was hard for them to talk much. Still, I think that Jason forgave his father. And I know that he was sorry. His last words were, 'I'm sorry.'"

Now I am sobbing again and it feels like I won't ever be able to stop. It's just so sad and it hurts so bad. Why did this happen?

Finally we both stop crying and I feel like I've been run over by one of those big rollers that they use to press the blacktop flat and smooth. It's like I'm just empty.

"I'm sorry," says Mrs. Harding. "I probably shouldn't have told you all that. Gary didn't want to tell anyone the details. Out of respect for Jason, we had meant to keep everything as quiet as possible. That's why we've made no comments to the news."

For some reason this bugs me. "But why?" I ask.

She looks somewhat confused. "I'm not sure exactly. But Gary thought it was best. The less people know about it, the better."

Okay, I might be sticking my foot into it now, but I have to say this. "I think that's wrong."

She blinks. "Wrong?"

"Yes. And I'll tell you why." So I explain to her about the suicide pact and how even though I've come to my senses, there are others who haven't, including her own neighbor Seth Blum.

"Oh dear."

I nod. "I think you have a responsibility to make this known. I mean, the part about how Jason regretted his choice and how he didn't actually think he was going to die from the overdose. Otherwise, there could be other kids who will imitate him and—"

"You're absolutely right, Morgan. But I wonder how I should do it."

"I suppose you could make a statement to the media," I begin. "But it might have even more impact if this was mentioned at the memorial service tomorrow."

"Do you really think so?"

"I don't know, Mrs. Harding. But I guess I'm trying to think of what Jason would want. And I don't think he'd want his friends to go killing themselves like copycats. I think he'd do everything possible to prevent it."

"Yes, I think you're right." She looks confused now. "But how do I go about this?"

Somehow we manage to come up with a plan, but it's up to me to carry it out.

nineteen

I GO STRAIGHT HOME AND CALL THE CHURCH TO SEE IF MARCUS IS THERE but I'm told that he's already gone home. And so I call his home and get Tracie.

"I'm so glad to hear your voice," she tells me. "We've really been praying for you."

"Thanks," I say. "Maybe it's helping. I've just been at Jason's house talking to Mrs. Harding, and there's something I need to tell Marcus. It's really important. Is he there?"

"Not yet. But he should be home any minute. Do you want to call back? Or you could come over. We'd both love to see you. How about coming for dinner tonight?"

And so it's settled. As soon as Mom gets home, I borrow her car and drive over to the Nickersons'. I am barely through the front door of their house when I begin to feel a little better. I think I've forgotten how good it is to be in their home. The way that Tracie has it decorated, like Pottery Barn meets funky garage sale, and the music they usually have playing . . . well, the whole thing just feels so right. It's the way I want to have my own home someday. Someday a long time from now.

I decide not to tell them too much about Jason while we're having dinner. But I do let them know that I'm back in a relationship with God. "And this time it's for the long haul," I say. "Your talk really got to me last Sunday, Marcus. Talk about hitting the nail on the head. And I've been praying and reading my Bible again. And this time it seems more powerful than before." I can tell Marcus is really happy about this, but fortunately he's too smooth to gush or do anything embarrassing like that.

Just as we're finishing dinner, I begin telling them the truth about Jason. And to my surprise, I don't feel nearly as sad telling this story as I did hearing it.

"He really didn't *want* to die?" asks Tracie as she begins to clear the table.

"No," I say as I get up to help her. "He just wanted to get his parents' attention."

"That is so sad," says Marcus as he picks up some serving dishes and follows us into the kitchen. "I mean, it's sad no matter how you look at it, but to think that he never meant to really carry it out, and then it was too late. Man, that is *so* sad."

"Yeah," I agree. "That's how I felt at first. But now I'm seeing it a little differently."

"How's that?" asks Tracie as she rinses a plate.

"Well, I'm just so relieved to know that he didn't really want to end his own life. You know? Because, honestly, when I heard that Jason committed suicide . . . well, it's like my own life got totally dark and black and hopeless. Like, if Jason couldn't take it anymore, how could someone like me survive? Do you know what I mean?"

"Kind of," says Tracie.

"I get you," says Marcus. And I know he does. "I mean, we all make dumb choices sometimes. But it's like Jason wasn't really making the choice to end his life that day. It seems more like he was just crying out for help—help so that he could live his life. Don't you think that's it?"

"I do," I say as I hand Tracie another plate.

"I see what you're saying," she says.

"But no one really knows about that," I say. "And his death is stirring up a lot of problems." Then I go ahead and tell them about the suicide pact I'd been in with Seth and Grace. I'm embarrassed to admit that I was part of it, but I feel like I need to come clean with these guys.

"Oh, Morgan!" says Tracie as she wipes her hands on a towel and then hugs me. "I'm so glad that you didn't go through with it! Oh, I would've been so upset. First Jason and then you. I don't know if our church could take that much pain."

I nod. "I know. I'm really sorry and actually kind of embarrassed that I got that low."

"But I can understand it," she says. "I mean, without allowing God to give you strength, and then losing your good friend. Wow, that's pretty depressing."

"Your grandma sounds like an angel to me," says Marcus as he puts the last plate into the dishwasher. "What perfect timing."

"Yeah. At the time I was mad. But then later I was relieved. Now I am totally thankful."

"But you're still worried about the other two? Seth and Grace?"

"And not just them." So I tell them how other kids are considering this same thing now and how we put the name box by the office. "I just hope it's enough."

"Someone should tell their parents," says Tracie as we go back into the living room.

"I think the box is helping with that," I say. "Even so, I think there's more to do." Then I tell them about my idea to talk about what really happened to Jason at the memorial service tomorrow. "Mrs. Harding asked me to see if you'd be willing."

"So his family's okay with this?" asks Marcus.

"She said that she'll be talking to them today. But she agreed that if it saved lives it would be worth it."

"Maybe I'll give them a call later," says Marcus.

"That'd probably be good."

We visit some more, but then I know that it's time for me to go. "Thanks for having me over," I tell them. "You have no idea how good it feels to be in your home."

"Come over anytime," says Tracie, and I think she means it. "We love having you here."

Then I go home. As I drive across town I pray, once again, for Seth and Grace, and now Micah too. I pray that Marcus will say something tomorrow that will make a difference for them or that God will send them angels to stop them, the same way he sent my grandma.

I'm barely in the house when I hear the phone ringing. Since my mom and Grandma are sitting on the couch, I make the dash to pick it up and am surprised to hear Grace's voice.

I take the cordless to my room and ask her how she's doing.

"Not good," she says.

"What's going on?"

"Seth just called."

"And?"

"And, oh, I don't know. He's pretty convincing, Morgan. After talking to him I just feel like giving up, like what's the use anyway? What difference does it make whether I live or die? And wouldn't dying be a whole lot easier than this?"

"But don't you remember what we talked about, Grace? About how you can't take it back once it's done?"

"Yeah, and I tried to explain that to Seth. But it's like he's the expert or something. And he always has so many reasons—reasons that really make sense."

Then I tell her what Jason's mom told me and I can tell by the silence on the other end that I have her full attention.

"Seriously?" she finally says. "Is that really true?"

"Mrs. Harding told me herself."

"You mean he didn't really want to—" she chokes up. "He didn't *want* to die?"

"No. It was only to get their attention."

Now all I can hear is quiet sobs. But I just wait, praying as I do.

"Grace?" I finally say.

"Yeah?"

"Can't you see what this means?"

"Not really."

"Well, do you honestly think Jason would want us to follow his example when he didn't even mean to do it himself?"

"I don't know."

"Well, think about it, Grace. Maybe it takes time for it to sink in. But really, just think about it."

"Yeah. I will."

"Can you imagine how bad he would feel to think that his mistake cost more lives? Lives of people he loved? Don't you think that would make him sad?"

"I guess. But, Morgan, where do you think he is? I mean, really."

"Honestly?"

"Yeah, honestly."

"I think he's in heaven."

"So you really believe in heaven?"

I consider this. I mean, it's not like I have any real image of what heaven will look like or feel like, but how can I believe in God without believing in heaven? "Yeah," I finally say. "I do."

"But if that's true, if he killed himself and went to heaven, then why couldn't we all just do the same?"

"I don't know the answer to that, Grace. But here's what I think: I think he didn't *mean* to do it. That he made a stupid choice because of what was going on in his life right then. And that he only meant to get his dad's attention."

"Yeah, well, he accomplished that."

"But it cost him everything, Grace. And he wasn't even ready to go."

"But you think he's in heaven?"

I pause to consider this again. And I have to admit that there's a real sense of peace inside me, something that convinces me that heaven is real. "Yeah, I really do."

"It's kind of mind-boggling to me. I mean, I don't know if I even believe in heaven or God or anything."

"Well, I can tell you this: My life is way more worthwhile when I do believe in those things. I don't think I can live without God." And even as I say these words, I remember something. "Hey, that's exactly what Jason used to say to me!"

"Yeah, I remember him saying that too."

"So, see," I say, "he *must* be in heaven."

"Maybe." But she doesn't sound convinced.

"Well, just think about it. See you tomorrow then?"

"Yeah. See ya."

twenty

I'M JUST GETTING READY FOR BED WHEN I HEAR THE PHONE RING AGAIN. Then Mom brings it and says it's for me. Now, under normal circumstances, she would be seriously annoyed at me for getting a call this late, but she seems to understand that this is not a normal time for anyone.

I am surprised that it's Grace again. "What's up?" I ask.

"I thought I should tell you something," she says. "It's really been bugging me and I didn't know who else to tell."

"What is it?"

"There are more kids."

I wait, but she doesn't say anything. "More kids?" I repeat.

"Who want to do it."

"You mean kill themselves? They've joined the suicide pact?"

"Yeah, whatever you want to call it. But Seth told me there are about seven who are really serious."

I feel my heart sinking. "Did he give you names?"

"Yeah. But I didn't know all of them. And he didn't give last names for everyone."

"Can you remember who they are?" I ask as I reach for my notebook and pen. "I'm guessing Micah is one."

"Yeah," she says. And then she gives me the other names and

I write them all down.

"Thanks," I tell her. "Does this mean you've decided not to go through with it?"

"Yeah, I guess. I think maybe I'm starting to see that it's not the answer." She pauses. "And if it's okay, I'd like to talk to you some more. I have some questions . . . you know, about God and stuff."

"Yeah, definitely," I assure her. "Anytime."

"Well, thanks."

As soon as we hang up, I go online. I still have Detective Mason's business card with his e-mail address, and I decide to e-mail him this list of names, as well as tell him that their plans to attempt this after the funeral service tomorrow are still on.

Then while I'm online, I decide to do a quick search on Tylenol and suicide in general. I type in some search words and am surprised to learn that this method is actually quite common, especially among teens. I read and read and become pretty distressed by what I learn. I've never heard of most of this information, never seen it reported either on the news or in the paper.

Somebody ought to make this stuff known. And since I'm a writer for the school newspaper and I don't have anything for this week's edition, I decide to write an article about teen suicide and Tylenol and dedicate it to Jason. The paper comes out on Friday and my deadline isn't until Wednesday afternoon, but I make a good start on the article before I'm too exhausted to even think coherently. Then I remind myself that tomorrow's another day—and a busy one at that—so I go to bed.

I get up early the next morning, since I plan to go straight to the photo lab and make enlargements of Jason's pictures before class starts. I've got a final before lunch and can't skip that. To my relief, Mr. Spencer is there and he helps walk me through the process.

"That's sure nice of you to do this," he says as we wait for them to print.

"I plan to pay for the materials," I tell him.

"No," he says. "Jason was well-loved in this department. Why don't you let us take care of that? Besides, it's pretty minimal."

"Thanks." I consider mentioning my use of the yearbook film but stop myself. I can take care of that later.

"Do you have anything to frame or mat these photos with?" he asks as he holds one up.

"I didn't really think about that."

"Do you know anyone in the art department?"

"Sure, my best friend, Carlie, is pretty involved in art."

"Why don't you give her the dimensions of the photos and see what she can do for you?"

"Great idea."

"I can finish these up," he tells me.

So I go off in search of Carlie and by nine o'clock we have beautiful black-and-white photographs of Jason that are expertly matted and backed.

The school has postponed the afternoon finals and allowed anyone who wants to attend Jason's funeral to take off after lunch. With Carlie's permission, I invite Grace to ride with us after my English exam—if I passed, it will be a miracle—and we all head over to the church.

The Hardings are already there. Mr. Harding and Aaron are off to one side, quietly talking with Pastor Orlander. Their faces look serious and I wonder if they're talking about what Marcus can or cannot say. Mrs. Harding is sitting with her daughter in the front pew. Feeling a little uneasy, I make my way toward the front of the sanctuary, where Mrs. Harding sees me.

"Hello, Morgan," she says as she stands and moves toward me. "These must be the pictures of Jason!" And so I show them to her and suddenly Jason's family and Pastor Orlander are looking at the enlarged photos and making positive comments.

"These are really great," says Jason's sister, Jessica. "I didn't know you were such a photographer, Morgan." She smiles sadly at me. "But then, you've grown up quite a bit since the last time I saw you."

I nod. "Yeah. I guess we all have."

"I'll put them up on the easels," says Aaron as he carefully takes all three of the bulky photos from me.

"We've got a couple of Jason's senior pictures too," says Mrs. Harding, nodding toward the front. Then in a quieter voice she says, "But I think yours are better."

I glance up to the pulpit area. I've never seen it so colorful. Flowers seem to be everywhere, but then that should be no surprise when you consider that Mrs. Harding runs a florist's shop. I see Jason's senior photos and, while they are nice enough, I don't think they capture the same qualities that mine do. But then I'm probably biased. Mostly I'm glad that I took those photos when I did. And to think it had only been to use up the roll of film so I could develop some shots for the paper.

I thank Mrs. Harding, then start to go, but she places a hand on my arm. "Please, Morgan, won't you sit with us?"

I glance back to where Carlie and Grace are already sitting a few rows back, but they both nod at me like they understand and it's okay. "Sure," I tell Mrs. Harding. "I'd be honored to sit with you."

I go into the pew first so that I will be on the far end. I just don't feel right sitting between the family members. Besides, I'm not too sure how the others might feel about me being here. I always felt like the poor kid from the wrong side of the tracks around them.

But now I'm wondering if maybe I just imagined the whole thing, because they all seem to be treating me nicely. Jessica follows me into the pew, sitting beside me, and then her mother comes. I'd like to ask Mrs. Harding how her family responded to the idea of bringing the truth to light during Jason's memorial service. But somehow I can't bring myself to lean across Jessica to ask about something that may be highly sensitive.

Instead I just look down at my lap and pray. I pray that God will do a miracle in here today. I pray that Marcus has received the family's blessing to tell Jason's story and will be able to reach kids like Seth and Micah and the others with just the right words. Before long, I hear music and the service is beginning.

I look up to see Mrs. Pointer, the organist. Her head is bent over the keyboard as she quietly plays a hymn. And that's when I notice it. For the first time I see it. Up there, surrounded by flowers, with the photos in front, I see Jason's casket. And something about seeing that sleek-looking, stainless-steel casket and knowing that my dear friend's lifeless body is inside just totally unravels me and, once again, I begin to cry.

Jessica turns to look at me and, noticing that I haven't had the sense to bring tissues, she reaches in her purse (where she has a whole pack) and extracts one for me.

"Thanks," I mutter.

She pats me on the arm. "No problem."

"It's just so unreal," I whisper.

"Yeah." She nods looking up toward the front. "I know."

I try to stay focused on the words as Pastor Orlander speaks, but I can feel myself drifting in and out. Mostly I am thinking about Jason, thinking about all the good times we shared over the years and how much I love him and miss him.

"I believe Jason is looking down on us right now," says our pastor. This gets my attention. "Right this minute," he says, "I believe that he's with God the Father. And the reason I believe that is because our God, the great Redeemer, has already paid the price for Jason's redemption. That price was paid when Jesus Christ died on the cross for all of us. And that deal was sealed on the day that Jason allowed Jesus' death to give him eternal life. So, if anyone here has any doubts, any questions concerning Jason's status with God, I can assure you as his pastor that Jason is with God. Right now."

I return to fading in and out as he goes on, quoting Scriptures that support his belief. And it's not that I doubt him, because I don't. But even so, I feel bad. Because even though Jason's with God, he's not with me. He's gone. And I miss him. I'm sure that I will miss him for a long, long time. Maybe for my entire life. And it seems that no words of consolation can change that.

Jessica gives me another tissue and I notice that I am not the only one crying. In fact, it seems that everyone in the sanctuary, at least everyone I can see (which is only the first few rows) is crying.

But I think that may be a good thing. Maybe our tears will help heal us. And instead of feeling sorry for myself for losing Jason, I decide to refocus my energy by praying for the other kids from our school. I pray for the ones who are considering suicide and I pray for the ones who are just hurting, the ones who are confused about life and death and Jason's apparent choice to give up and end it all.

Then Pastor Orlander introduces Marcus and suddenly I am all ears. And I am praying again that he'll be able to speak freely.

"I know that many of you feel confused today," he begins. "I know how stunned I was the day I learned of Jason's death. It just made no sense to me." Then he goes on to tell about some of the things that he and Jason had done together and how Jason was such a vital part of the youth group. "And Jason's faith was real," he says. "He lived what he believed and I'm sure that many of you experienced that firsthand. I know this for a fact because many of you have called me to talk. And you've told me your own stories about how Jason touched your life. He was kind and generous and he always took time to listen to his friends. In some ways, Jason was one of the most Christlike guys I have known. And yet he took his own life, or so it seems, and that has left us feeling confused and torn and disillusioned.

"But I want to tell you something that you may not know, something that may change the way you perceive this young man's life and his death." He pauses now and the church grows very quiet. He's really got their attention.

"We recently learned, from Jason's own family, that he didn't really want to take his own life last week." He pauses again and looks evenly across the crowd. "But Jason made a mistake. A fatal mistake. Feeling the pressure and stress of everyday life, Jason was pushed to his limits, and in a cry for help and attention, he took an intentional overdose of pills. But because he really didn't want to die, he confessed his mistake and asked for help. And although his family and the medical staff did everything in their power to save him, *it was too late*. Too much time had lapsed and the poison that he'd ingested had already done its damage. And Jason died. But trust me, people, *he did not want to die*." He pauses again, sighing deeply before he continues. "And so what would Jason say to us if he were here today? I think he would tell us that no matter how hard it gets, we should never give up. I think he would tell us that he still wishes he were here with us. I think he would tell us that God is big enough to carry us through any troubles, and I think he would tell us that he blew it big-time when he took such drastic measures to express his frustrations about his life.

"Now, whether we believe in God or not, we all get discouraged from time to time. So don't be harsh in your judgment of Jason, because you could easily find yourself in his shoes. You could make the same mistake he did and be sorry later. Instead, let's learn from Jason. Let's remember that God is our help in times of trouble. Let's remember that if we lean on him, he can see us through. And let's remember that God gives us each other to help carry the load when the weight gets too heavy. I think that's what Jason would say to us today."

twenty-one

I NOTICE A LOT OF FAMILIAR FACES, AS WELL AS RED EYES, AS I EXIT THE church. But it's Detective Mason, standing near the front door, who gets my attention. There's another man standing with him, not in uniform, but I suspect he may be a policeman too. Detective Mason nods at me as I pass but says nothing. I think he must've received my e-mail. I also see Seth and Micah and the other kids whose names are on the list. But I have no idea what they're thinking right now or whether any of the things said here today have reached them. I can only pray.

Outside, I am joined by Grace and Carlie. We talk to some of our friends and then I notice the long gray hearse pulling out of the back parking lot. It's being followed by a couple of dark limos, which must be for the family. And then some other cars line up for the procession to the cemetery.

"Looks like it's time to go," says Carlie. "You guys ready?" I ride in the backseat with Grace, and while Carlie drives I can't believe the long train of cars that is slowly snaking through the city and making its way up to the cemetery. It's like something out of a movie.

Soon we are at the gravesite along with about a hundred other people. Then we wait as more cars come and more people trek up the path to where we are gathered. We're several rows back and although we can't see anything, I'm hoping we can hear. Mostly I just want to pray.

I am surprised to feel a hand tapping me on my shoulder and I look up to see Aaron, Jason's brother. "Mom asked me to invite you to come sit with the family," he says.

I glance at my friends and once again they all nod as if I should go. "Thanks," I tell Aaron, and I follow him up to the front and take a seat on the end of the row.

But now I am staring directly at the casket, wondering if I wouldn't have been better off in the back. I feel a giant lump growing in my throat and I just hope I can keep it together. It feels so final to see the casket and know that carpet of fake green grass is covering the hole it will go down into. It all just makes me feel so sad and hopeless again. Like this is it. There goes my friend. Never to be seen again. Over and out.

Okay, I do believe in God and I do believe in heaven. But for some reason it feels so far away to me right now, and I'll admit it, a little unreal. Now, the casket, the hole, the gravestone . . . those things look very real to me. Very final. Very unforgiving.

It seems that everyone is here now, and Pastor Orlander steps up beside the grave and begins to speak.

"Despite our sadness, this is a time to rejoice," he says in a strong voice. "And despite our attempts to elude death, we must all face it ourselves one day. For God gave us temporary bodies to take us through a temporary earthly life. But when our lives belong to God, when we are truly his, he rewards us with eternal life—and that lasts forever."

He looks up toward the sky. "And that's where Jason is right now. And while he might not have meant to arrive so soon, we trust that our heavenly Father has welcomed him in the same way that the father of the prodigal son welcomed his son—with open arms."

Then he opens his Bible and reads. "Death is swallowed up in victory. O Death, where is your sting? O Hades, where is your victory?" Then he closes it and leads us in another prayer.

He says a few more words and then, as we sing "Amazing Grace," Jason's casket is slowly lowered into the dark hole in the earth. And that's it. Everyone begins to leave. And I know it's time for me to go too. But it's like I'm frozen there, like I can't move my feet.

I come out of my daze when I notice Grace over by a pine tree. She's talking to Seth and I can tell by their expressions and hand motions that she's trying to explain her decision, but I can also tell that he's not buying it.

"I better go help Grace," I tell Carlie, who has come to stand beside me. "Do you mind waiting for us?"

"No problem."

So I walk over to where the two of them appear to be in some kind of standoff. "Hey, Seth," I say casually.

He ignores me, keeping his eyes fixed on Grace. "I can't believe you're buying into all that crap," he says. "Don't you remember how you told me that you were fed up with everything about this moronic existence? You said that life sucks. So when did that all change, Grace?"

"Nothing has changed about those things," she says. "Life does suck. At least it sucks right now. But like Morgan says, it might not suck next week or next month or next year. But if you kill yourself, you won't be around to see it get better. Don't you get that, Seth?"

He scowls now. "I get it." Then he turns and looks at me. "I get that you guys have both chickened out."

"No," I tell him. "You're the one who's chickening out, Seth. You're the one who's running away from your problems. The brave thing to do is to live. And Marcus Nickerson got it right when he said that's what Jason would tell us if he could."

"You honestly believe that?" he asks. "That Jason never meant to do it?"

"I do," I assure him. "Jason's own mom told me."

He swore. "Yeah, well, that explains everything, Morgan. You should know as well as anyone how that family is all about appearances. They'll look a lot better if they can lie and say their son really didn't *want* to do it. It was all just an accident. Yeah, you bet."

"Listen, Seth," I say. "They had never planned to disclose the truth. Mr. Harding was embarrassed because Jason had taken the pills to get his attention. Honestly, Mr. Harding did *not* want this to be known. It was Mrs. Harding who spilled the beans. And then I begged her to let everyone hear the truth."

Now Seth just shoves his hands into his pockets and stares down at the grass. I'm not sure whether he's really angry or actually thinking about all this.

"Look, Seth," I say quietly, noticing that we're drawing attention from the funeral goers. "Why don't we take this someplace more private?"

"Yeah," agrees Grace.

"Let's go over there," says Seth, and we all start walking to the other side of the cemetery.

"Wait!" I turn and see Micah walk over to our little group like he plans to join us. Apparently Carlie noticed him and decided to come too. Great, now everyone will think we're all going off to kill ourselves together. In the cemetery even. How appropriate.

"Hey, Micah," I say in an unenthusiastic tone as we start

trekking up a path toward some trees.

"Hey," he says in a glum voice with eyes downcast.

"You still serious about doing yourself in?" I ask him.

He almost smiles. Almost. Then he just frowns and shrugs. "I don't know."

Seth turns and looks at him. "Yeah, Micah's probably gonna chicken out on me too." He shakes his head. "Man, I might as well just do this thing solo."

"It's not about chickening out, Seth," Grace tells him. "Like Morgan said, it's a lot braver to live and face things than it is to take the easy way out."

"You mean what appears to be the easy way out," I say as we finally stop at a picnic table. I think that's pretty weird, like who would have a picnic in the cemetery? But at least it's more secluded in the trees and we've got a place to sit.

"But the truth is, none of us knows what comes next," adds Carlie as we sit down.

"Well, I'm gonna know," says Seth as he lights up a cigarette.

"And what if it turns out to be a big mistake?" I ask. "What if everything ends up way worse than what you've got right now? And what if you wish you'd never done it, but it's too late? You're stuck. No turning back."

"That's not how your preacher guys made it sound for Jason. According to them, Jason is having the time of his life right now."

"Jason was a Christian," says Carlie. "That makes a pretty huge difference, you know."

"So, what if I become a Christian too?" says Seth, and Micah actually laughs at this.

"Yeah, sure," says Micah. "That's a brilliant plan."

"You seriously think you can pull one over on God?" asks Carlie.

"Yeah, right," says Grace. "You better think this through a little better."

"Why?" asks Seth. "If I say I'm a Christian, who's to say I'm not?"

"God," I tell him. "He does know the difference."

"But you could give it a try," suggests Carlie. "I mean, you could invite Jesus into your heart. Then you could ask God if he thinks it's a good idea to kill yourself."

Now it feels like this whole thing is taking a bad twist. Not that I wouldn't love for Seth to find God. But the conversation is all wrong. And I can tell that Seth is getting mad and feeling defensive.

"Look," I say. "This is the thing. We all really like you, Seth. We would really like you to stick around. I mean, I've just barely gotten to know you again, and that's only been since Jason died. I think you're a cool guy with some pretty radical ideas, and I'd like to get to know you better."

"That's right," says Grace. "Think about it, Seth. Don't you think it's what Jason would want?"

"For you to kill yourself is kind of like a slap in Jason's face," says Carlie. "Especially knowing that Jason never really meant to die. It's almost like your death would be his fault."

"That's not true," says Seth. "It's not like Jason gave me the idea in the first place. I don't even know what's kept me from doing it all this time."

"Maybe it's God," says Carlie.

Seth swears.

"Seriously, Seth," says Carlie. "I've been praying for you and I think God has—"

"I don't want to hear about God!" he yells.

"What about Jason?" I ask him. "Do you want to hear about

Jason? Do you even care about what he'd try to say to you right now?"

"I don't know." Seth looks down at the table now. Then in a quieter voice he says, "It's just too hard."

"What's too hard?" I ask.

"To live," he says, his voice cracking. "It's too freaking hard to live!" Then he pounds his fist on the table. "And I can't take it anymore."

"That's because you're doing it all alone," I tell him. "And trust me, I know exactly how that feels. I mean, I had turned my back on God, and after Jason was gone, I felt so bad that I just wanted to end it all too. You saw how miserable I was, Seth. I had absolutely no hope. But then I gave my life back to God and things are starting to change. And I know that I don't want to kill myself after all."

"Well, good for you," says Seth. "Too bad it's not like that for the rest of us."

"It can be," says Carlie, "if you're willing to try. The problem is that you're not. You think you have it all figured out, Seth. But you don't know up from down. And if you kill yourself, your troubles will just be starting."

"Seth," says Grace, "can't you see that we've all been seriously depressed by Jason's death? But that we've all been figuring out that suicide won't fix anything?"

"Maybe that's true with you guys," he says. "But there are others who might still be willing to give it a try."

"Give it a *try*?" I echo. "Look, Seth, you don't *try* suicide. Once you do it, it's a done deal. And if you don't like it, that's too bad. Can't you see that? Death is a permanent condition."

"And look at how much Jason's death has hurt everyone," adds Grace. "Do you really want to be a source of pain for everyone?"

"Look, Seth," I begin, praying even as I speak. "Instead of having a pact to die, what if we had a *pact to live*? What if we did this for Jason's sake? Kind of like a memorial to honor him? What if we all agreed to stick together, to continue being friends, and to face life head-on?"

Seth is looking down at the table now. I'm not even sure he's listening.

"That's a cool idea, Morgan," says Grace. "A pact to live. I'm in."

"And we can keep hanging out together and we can talk about all these things," I say. "And maybe include others who are feeling confused too. But we have to make it clear that it's a *pact to live*. Right?"

"Right," says Micah. "I'm in."

"And even though I wasn't considering suicide, I'm in," says Carlie.

But Seth isn't saying anything. He's just sitting there like a stone, staring at the table, and I have no idea what he's thinking.

"Come on, Seth," urges Grace as she reaches across the table and puts her hand on his arm. "Can't you do this with us? For Jason?"

He looks up with tears in his eyes. "I don't know."

"You can do it," I tell him. "We'll help you. Just trust us, okay? We're your friends."

"That's right, man," says Micah. "We don't want to lose you. We've lost enough lately."

"And I've still got things I want to tell you," I continue. "And I need you to stick around so that I can." I am thinking about Marcus' challenge to commit spiritual suicide by dying to ourselves daily. Somehow I think Seth might get this. If he can just hold on and make it that far. In the meantime, I think he might need some serious help. Beyond what we can do for him.

"I don't know what to do," says Seth. And now the tears are running freely.

I glance across the table at Micah. "You rode here with Seth, right?"

He nods.

"Maybe you should drive him home and then we should meet you guys there."

"Why?" asks Seth as he wipes his nose with his hand.

"Because I think you need to let your parents know what's going on," I say, bracing myself for the worst. "And you need to be willing to get some help."

"I—uh—I don't know," he says. But already, Micah is helping him to his feet.

"Don't worry, man, we're here for you. We're going to walk you through this thing."

And so we pile back into our cars and head over to Seth's house. I notice there are a lot of cars parked on his street because of Jason's funeral. The Hardings are probably having family members over. And it's weird; now that I'm so focused on Seth, the whole thing with Jason feels a little less painful.

We park in Seth's driveway behind his car. And we all go inside, where Seth and the others wait in the family room while I go look for his mom. I find her in the kitchen and, naturally, she is surprised to see me. But her eyes look troubled, and I can tell she's been crying.

"I'm sorry to bother you," I say quickly. "But we brought Seth home. We did kind of an intervention thing with him." Then I explain, once again, about the suicide pact and she finally takes me seriously.

"Yes," she says. "The police have called, and it seems there are a number of kids involved and that Seth is the leader. They want to talk to him."

"He's still pretty upset and depressed," I tell her. "I think he needs some serious help. But I hate to leave him like this. We've all been talking to him and I think he trusts us, you know?"

"Yes." She nods and moves to the phone. "Why don't you all stay with him and I'll make some phone calls."

So I go back to the living room and sit with my friends. Carlie and Grace are sitting on either side of Seth on the sectional, and he's hunched over like a puppet whose strings have been cut. I feel so bad for him.

"Everything's going to be okay," Micah is saying. "Just hang in there, man."

I sit next to Micah and nod. "Yeah, Seth, I talked to your mom and she totally understands. She needed to make some phone calls and then she'll be in here."

Grace is rubbing his back. "You're going to feel better," she assures him. "It just takes time."

It's not long before Detective Mason and a psychiatrist arrive. They briefly question Seth, and to my relief, he is honest with them and the doctor decides to take him in for treatment and observation. And Seth doesn't even disagree.

"Thank you all for coming," says Mrs. Blum. "We really appreciate it."

"We care about Seth," I tell her. "We know how he feels and we just want him to get better."

twenty-two

I LEARN LATER, THROUGH DETECTIVE MASON, THAT THE SUICIDE PACT HAS been averted. "You kids were instrumental," he tells me by phone. "You have no idea how much we appreciate your cooperation with us."

"I'm just glad that it's over."

"It's never completely over," he says in a sad voice. "Unfortunately, suicide is still the second-highest cause of death among teens."

"Well, I guess I mean for now. At least it's over for now, right?"

"Right. As far as we know. But I hope you kids will keep watching out for each other," he says, "because you have the inside scoop when it comes to your friends and how they're coping with life. Even the parents are out of the loop."

"Yeah," I tell him. "Hopefully we can all learn how to be better friends from this."

I barely hang up the phone when I am assaulted by a boatload of guilt. I know I wasn't that good a friend to Jason. I can't deny it. I blew it and I blew it bad. But I can't keep dwelling on this mistake either. And so, once again, I give my heartache to God. I tell him, again, that I am so sorry and I thank him for forgiving me. And this time I ask him to help me forgive myself. This is just too heavy a load to keep carrying all by myself.

Then I go back to writing my article for the school paper. I know I need to turn it in tomorrow and I hope to finish it before I go to bed tonight.

It's nearly midnight by the time I'm done, but I think staying up was worth it. I think that I said some things in there that might make a difference, might make kids think twice before they decide to throw in the towel permanently. At least I hope so.

***

By Friday, it seems like everyone at school has finally settled down and is moving on. I feel relieved to see that the shrine at Jason's locker has been removed. I had gotten to the place where I would go out of my way just to avoid it. Not that I didn't want to be reminded of Jason, that's not it. But seeing that stuff piled around his locker only seemed to magnify the fact that he is no longer with us. I don't need that.

"Seth is coming home tomorrow," Micah announces to us at lunch. We've been sitting together in the cafeteria this week—our pact-to-live group. I guess it's kind of like group therapy. But it's working. I know that I'm totally thankful to be surrounded by friends who actually get it. I mean, they know how I feel, but they don't always try to say something to make me feel better. Because it's just not like that. And I've been surprised at how our numbers have steadily increased as the word got out. I guess we're kind of like survivors or something. Anyway, I don't think I've ever had this many friends before. And I guess I have Jason to thank for that.

"Do you think we should do something for Seth?" I ask the group. "I mean, to make it easier for him to come home, you know?"

"Yeah, I was thinking about that," says Micah. "It'd be cool for him to know that we're still backing him, still his friends."

"Our youth group is having bowling night at the Super Pit on Saturday," says Carlie. "I know it sounds corny, but it's actually pretty fun."

"And they have miniature golf too," I offer.

"I think that sounds great," says Grace. "I for one am ready to lighten up a little."

"And everyone can come," says Carlie to the rest of the group. "It's for anyone in high school."

And so it's settled. We will welcome Seth back into the land of the living with something as down-to-earth as bowling and putting. Hey, it works for me.

The newspaper comes out today, and I feel a little nervous about that. I'm not sure how people will respond to my article about suicide. But I take some comfort in knowing I said what needed to be said.

When the newspapers come out at the end of fifth period, like they always do, I get one and go straight to the restroom and go into a stall and close the door so I can read it undisturbed. But first I read a touching memorial written by Mr. Spencer for Jason. It's titled "A Hero Passes." The article talks about who Jason really was—a hard worker, a good listener, a diligent student, a loyal friend, and someone who liked to laugh. "A real hero," it says, "is someone who can never be measured by trophies or plaques or even prestigious scholarships. True heroism can only be measured by the heart. . . ."

I can't believe how well Mr. Spencer has nailed it. But then Jason had spent a fair amount of time in the journalism department. And he'd obviously had an influence, even on Mr. Spencer's life. I'll have to remember to get an extra copy of this paper to take to the Hardings. I think Jason's mother would enjoy reading this one. Probably a lot more than the last one I took her.

Next I go to my article. I tell myself that I only want to see how Mr. Spencer edited it, but I know I need to read the words once more. To see if they make as much sense now as they did when I so feverishly wrote it.

What You Don't Know Can Kill You
Morgan Bergstrom

The suicide rate among teens is higher than ever before, making it the second most common cause of death in our age group. But if that's not alarming enough, some of these so-called "suicides" are nothing more than the tragic results of misinformation.

Many teens, thinking they will get the attention they so desperately need, will swig down a bottle of pills, often ingesting something straight from the family medicine cabinet. With most pills, the person will immediately begin to experience symptoms like severe nausea or stomach cramps. This frightening pain often alarms the teens, causing them to call for help and wind up in a hospital where medical attention can save their lives.

This is not the case with acetaminophen. Commonly packaged under the brand name Tylenol, this innocent-looking pill promises to be "gentle on the stomach." So gentle, in fact, that the overdose victim can go for hours before he or she starts feeling ill. And by then it is too late.

Such was the fate of our good friend Jason Harding. Depressed and distressed over personal issues, Jason downed a full bottle of Tylenol pills early

Thursday morning. Then, feeling perfectly normal, he actually came to school for a few hours. With a lethal dose of acetaminophen in his stomach, Jason walked and talked among us, acting as if nothing whatsoever was wrong. And none of us had the slightest clue as to what was going on inside him. Perhaps Jason didn't either.

I have to admit that my first reaction to the news that Jason died from an overdose of Tylenol was one of disbelief. Seriously, I didn't understand how someone could die from something so seemingly harmless as Tylenol. It made no sense.

Research informed me better. I learned that 75 percent of teens attempting suicide reach for the medicine cabinet, and about half of them go for something as common and seemingly innocent as Tylenol. However, we don't know what they're thinking as they consume those pills — whether they are seriously wanting to die or just crying out for help. Perhaps we will never know.

But at least we will know this: If you take an overdose of Tylenol and feel no symptoms, don't assume that everything's okay. It's not. One researcher compares Tylenol to bleach. A little bit of bleach, diluted with water, can get your laundry clean. But if you use too much bleach, the fabric will fall apart and disintegrate. This is the same with Tylenol. A proper dosage won't hurt you, but when you take an overdose it will literally dissolve your liver and vital organs — so that you cannot possibly survive. Only it won't be a quick death, and you won't simply fall asleep. Once the pills take effect, up to 24 hours later, you will be in severe pain and misery right up until the end. But it will be the end.

So if you think you're taking the easy way out by chugging down pills, think again. But even more than that, you'd better rethink suicide altogether. Because, not unlike acetaminophen poisoning, suicide is irreversible and it is permanent. No matter how bad you feel today, things can and probably will get better tomorrow. And the world will be a better place if you are still in it.

If you or someone you know is considering checking out for good, tell someone right now. Get the help and attention needed — before it's too late.

Some of the symptoms of a person who may be considering suicide are depression, change in eating or sleeping habits, drug or alcohol abuse, neglect of appearance, withdrawal from friends, boredom, loss of interest, and personality change.

While we cannot bring Jason Harding back, we can honor his memory by helping each other, by accepting our differences, and by living our lives to the fullest.

I fold the paper and sigh. I realize I didn't address everything about suicide in this article. But maybe it's a start. Maybe I'll write a follow-up article for the next edition.

twenty-three

It's Saturday now, the first official day of spring break — and exactly one week since the day I thought I was going to kill myself. That seems incredible to me as I pedal my bike downtown to pick up my prints. And yet I vividly remember that day. I remember how I rode around town, taking photos of everything and anything that I thought was worthwhile or of interest. And I remember how I actually sort of enjoyed myself that day, despite the fact that I was fairly certain it would be my last day alive. And now I thank God that it was not.

The old Loco-Photo guy isn't here today, but he was right about the cost. The total is just a little less than a hundred dollars and I suddenly wonder why I even bothered. I could've just thrown the whole mess away. What a waste!

Without looking at the prints, I get on my bike and head back home, where I go straight to my room and take out the glossy black-and-white photos and flip through the stacks, separating them into two piles. One pile I'd call pretty crappy and the other not so bad. And in the not-so-bad pile I notice that I've actually got some pretty good shots, shots I don't even remember taking. But then again, it was supposed to be the last day of my life. I'm sure that I missed a thing or two. One shot really grabs my attention. It's of a little girl who's maybe two or three and she's squatting down on the sidewalk. When I snapped it I just thought she looked kind of cute all hunched down like that. But now I see that she's looking at something. She is captivated by a flower that's growing between the cracks in the sidewalk. And for some reason this photo feels like a reminder of something, something important, like life is all around us, popping up in the most unexpected places if we'll only take time to look.

As I study these photos I remember my bizarre book idea, the one I thought would make my mom rich, and I begin to jot down some notes, just little things describing how I felt that day (assuming it was my last) or how I responded to things I saw (thinking I would never see them again). But to my surprise this crazy little project is really growing into something kind of interesting. At least to me. I temporarily title my pile of photos and notes "The Last Day of the Rest of My Life" and then promise myself that I will get back to it, maybe even finish it during spring break, but not right now.

I take my backpack and get back onto my bike and head across town again. This time I go up the road that leads to the cemetery. I have something I need to take care of.

I am completely out of breath by the time I pedal to the top of the hill, and so I get off and walk my bike down the trail that leads to Jason's grave. It's easy to spot from here because it's still covered with all kinds of floral arrangements. And when I get closer I can see that other kids have been up here and placed some of the same kinds of items that had been next to his locker.

I'm thankful that no one is up here right now, and I sit down on the ground next to his grave and then open my backpack and take out a copy of last week's newspaper. I straighten it out, then stick it beneath a wreath of slightly wilted yellow roses. I'm not even sure why I feel so compelled to do this, but I just do.

"I wrote that for you, Jason," I say quietly, looking over my shoulder just to make sure that no one's around to hear me. "I wish I had written it a couple of weeks earlier," I say. "And that you had read it and that it would've made a difference. But it's too late for that now."

I take in a deep breath and close my eyes. "But that's not why I came up here today," I say. "I came up here to say that I'm sorry. I'm really, really sorry. I know that I've said it before, but I feel like I need to say it again. Jason, I am so sorry that I wasn't a better friend to you. I'm sorry that I never saw this coming, that I didn't notice how stressed out you had been, that I didn't respond to your e-mail that day. And, as sorry as I am, I realize that there's nothing I can do about it now. Not as far as you are concerned. But I promise you, I will do this: I will try to be the best friend that I can from now on. I'll try to follow your example and love and accept others for who they are. And I will try to write the kind of things for the school paper that you would appreciate. I will not let your death be wasted, Jason. I will remember you always."

I'm crying again. But it's not those old wrenching, straight from the gut, painful kind of tears. These tears feel more like they are sealing something inside of me. Maybe it's the promise I am making to Jason.

Then as I stand up to leave, I realize that something else has happened just now. I realize that I've finally forgiven myself. And as I get on my bike, I thank God for helping me reach this place, because I know I couldn't have made it here on my own.

And as I coast down the hill toward town, I thank God that I am still alive and that he is still God and that life is still worth living.

reader's guide

1. Morgan was shattered by the news of Jason's death. How would you react under similar circumstances?

2. Was it right for Morgan to blame herself for Jason's suicide? Why or why not?

3. Why do you think Morgan got pulled into a suicide pact?

4. Why do you think Seth was so convinced that suicide was the answer?

5. Do you know anyone like Seth? Why do you think he was so depressed? What could help him?

6. Do you think that suicide is right under any circumstances? Why or why not?

7. Do you think you would be able to recognize the signs if someone you know was considering suicide? What would you say to that person?

8. What would you do if you or someone you knew was considering suicide? Would you tell anyone?

9. What does it mean to die to self daily for Christ?

10. What is it that makes you want to live?

For additional information about suicide and suicide prevention, visit http://www.suicidehelplines.org/

Burnt Orange

Coming in January 2005

So what's the big deal about one little drink anyway?

One

"HELLO, MY NAME IS AMBER CONRAD," I SAY IN MY MOST SERIOUS VOICE, "and *I am an alcoholic.*" I'm standing behind the podium in the front of the room, wearing a new T-shirt and a deadpan expression. "And I have to admit that I need serious help—"

Suddenly my friends burst out laughing and, of course, I can't help but laugh too. I step away from the wooden podium and head over to the kitchen area to help Simi and Lisa. It's actually youth group night and the three of us got here early because we're in charge of setting up snacks.

"Hey, I *never* accused you of being an alcoholic," says Simi Gartolini in a slightly defensive tone as she fills a bowl with cheese twists. Simi is my best friend who sometimes makes me crazy. "I only said I was concerned that you went to a drinking party last night."

"Yeah," says Lisa Chan as she arranges soft drink cans into a cooler full of ice. "What's up with that, Amber?"

"I think you guys are just jealous," I say, hoping I can change the subject from drinking to something a little more comfortable. "I think you're picking on me just because you two didn't get an invite to Tommy Campbell's party."

"Tommy Campbell's a snob and a moron." Simi makes a face as she pops a bright orange cheese twist into her mouth. "I don't even know why you think he's so cool anyway."

"Ooh," I say to Simi. "Sounding pretty judgmental for a Christian, don't ya think?" Then I grab a bag of tortilla chips and attempt to open it, finally resorting to using my teeth to rip the stubborn package.

"I just think God expects us to have some common sense," she says. "And I think your dad does too."

"Yeah," adds Lisa. "Going to that party was a dumb move, Amber. I mean, kids look up to us as Christians. We're supposed to be the leaders within our youth group. Seriously, what's going to happen when word gets around that Amber Conrad, daughter of Pastor Conrad, is a beer-drinking party girl?"

"Man, I never should've told you guys," I say to them. "And like I said, I only had one beer and I didn't even drink the whole thing. Seriously, it's no big deal. The only reason I was there at all was just so I could witness to Claire Phillips—"

"Yeah, you bet," says Simi. "That's a great idea, Amber, go to a drinking party, have a beer, and then witness to someone."

Lisa laughs. "Yeah, brilliant plan. Maybe you should share your strategies with youth group tonight."

Okay, now I'm feeling pretty defensive. I mean, what right do these two have to judge me and everyone else on the planet for that matter? Like, who made these two God?

"Whatever," I finally say as if I don't really care. "Think what you like about me," I tell them in a slightly wounded tone. Then I hear the sound of voices coming down the hallway toward us. "But hey, you don't have to tell everyone in youth group," I say quickly.

"You don't think they'll hear about it anyway?" asks Simi.

"I don't see why." Then I get more serious. "Come on, you guys," I plead with them. "Don't make this into a big deal, okay? I mean, I trusted you with this. I thought you were my friends."

Simi smiles now. "Okay, Amber. My lips are sealed."

"Yeah, mine too," says Lisa. "You happy now?"

I shrug. "I appreciate it." Oh, I know they're right; I probably won't be able to keep a lid on the fact that I went to Tommy's party last night anyway. I know as well as anyone how rumors fly through the information mill at Franklin High. But usually the rumors are about someone else. I don't think there's ever been a rumor about me personally. Of course, now that I'm a senior and graduation is only two months away, well, maybe I don't really care. I mean, hey, maybe it's about time!

And then the room starts filling up with youth group kids and I'm not so sure anymore. Do I really want these guys to know what I was up to last night? I mean, these are kids I have known for years. Kids whose parents are good friends with my parents. And, for the most part, they're nice kids. I mean, I know that everyone has their problems and stuff, and nobody's perfect, but these are the kinds of kids who really try to follow God and live their lives for his glory. And for the most part they are my friends. But the truth is, I actually think they're just a little bit boring. Maybe I think this more tonight than usual. But, of course, I don't let this show.

Instead, I smile and say "hey" to everyone, just like always. I even compliment Tyler Addison on his haircut, although I honestly think it's way too short for his long and narrow head. In fact, he kind of looks like Homer Simpson now. And I ask Laney Edwards if she's lost weight and, of course, this makes her smile. The truth is, she looks heavier than ever, and that fluffy hot-pink sweater isn't helping one bit.

Okay, I'll admit it, I'm a total hypocrite sometimes. But it's like I'm supposed to have this happy-face outlook on life all the time. Like I'm supposed to make everyone feel good about themselves, even if I'm telling a big fat lie. It's just how a pastor's family is supposed to act, you know.

Oh, sure, my parents never actually say as much. In fact, I'm pretty sure my dad would deny that he acts like that at all. Which, in my opinion, is just another falsehood. Okay, in defense of my well-meaning parents, I think maybe they actually sort of believe the outrageous things they say. It's like they've been doing it for so long they can't even tell the difference between the truth and phony baloney.

Anyway, I've studied them over the years, and I've learned from them as they play their funny little feel-good game without ever thinking twice. They just smile and tell their little white lies and act like it's no big deal. And, naturally, being a good daughter, I just follow their lead and do the same.

That's probably what got Claire Phillips' attention last week. It looked like she was having a bad day and I complimented her on her outfit, which, though probably expensive, didn't really look that great on her. I mean, it actually made her look stockier than she is. Not that she's exactly chubby, but she's kind of short and compact. Of course, it's the kind of curvy compactness that guys seem to like. Including her boyfriend, Tommy Campbell.

"Thanks, Amber," she said with a bright smile. Then she asked if I had my notes from English Lit on me.

"Sure," I told her. "Do you want to borrow them? I noticed you missed class yesterday."

"Yeah, I had a dentist appointment," she said. "But I don't want to get behind in that class. Mr. Emerson is hard enough on us as it is."

"Man, I know," I confessed. "He gave me a C for midterms."

"You got a C?" Her eyes grew wide.

"Yeah, and when I asked him why, he said it was to push me harder for the final grade. Can you believe it? And I've really been trying to keep my GPA up."

"Man, that sucks," she said as I handed her my notes. "I'll get these back to you in time for class," she promised.

Okay, I should know better than to loan out my notes, but for some reason I trusted Claire. And, all right, she's one of the most popular girls in our class and I wouldn't mind if she liked me better. And so I was pleasantly surprised when she returned my notes, in perfect condition I might add, and then actually invited me to Tommy's party.

"I can invite whoever I want," she assured me as we walked into Mr. Emerson's class. "So, I hope you'll come, Amber. I'd really like to see you there." Then she laughed. "And everyone knows Tommy's parties are the best."

I blinked and tried not to look too surprised, then I told her I'd think about it. By the end of class she'd already written down his address and phone number on a torn-off piece of paper. "Here," she said. "Now, seriously, I want you to come. Okay?"

"Okay," I said, then added, "I mean, I'll think about it."

"Good." She smiled. "Don't forget there are only two months

until graduation. And I've been trying to get to know more kids, you know, so I'll know more people at our reunions."

Now I had to laugh at that. "I guess I haven't been thinking that far ahead," I admitted.

She grinned. "Well, maybe you should."

And that's how I ended up going to Tommy Campbell's party. And, here's the truth, I actually had fun. And it wasn't boring at all. And Claire was really nice to me, and her other friends were nice too. And it's like everyone just really cut loose and had a great time. Sure, some kids drank too much and one girl even got sick and threw up in Tommy's pool, which really put a damper on swimming.

But I didn't get drunk and I didn't get sick. Mostly, I just had an unexpectedly fun time. And, really, what is wrong with that? I mean, even Jesus drank wine with his friends. And wasn't his first miracle turning water into wine? So, seriously, what is the problem?

about the author

MELODY CARLSON has written dozens of books for all age groups, but she particularly enjoys writing for teens. Perhaps this is because her own teen years remain so vivid in her memory. After claiming to be an atheist at the ripe old age of twelve, she later surrendered her heart to Jesus and has been following him ever since. Her hope and prayer for all her readers is that each one would be touched by God in a special way through her stories. For more information, please visit Melody's website at www.melodycarlson.com.